Praise
The Cranberry Cove Mysteries

"Peg Cochran has a truly entertaining writing style that is filled with humor, mystery, fun, and intrigue. You cannot ask for a lot more in a super cozy!"

—Open Book Society

"A fun whodunnit with quirky characters and a satisfying mystery. This new series is as sweet and sharp as the heroine's cranberry salsa."

—Sofie Kelly, *New York Times* bestselling author of the Magical Cats Mysteries

"Cozy fans and foodies rejoice—there's a place just for you and it's called Cranberry Cove."

—Ellery Adams, *New York Times* bestselling author of the Supper Club Mysteries

"I can't wait for Monica's next tasty adventure—and I'm not just saying that because I covet her cranberry relish recipe."

—Victoria Abbott, national bestselling author of the Book Collector Mysteries

Books by Peg Cochran

The Cranberry Cove Mysteries

Berried Secrets
Berry the Hatchet
Dead and Berried
Berried at Sea
Berried in the Past
Berried Motives
Berry the Evidence
Berried Grievances
A Berry Suspicious Death
Where the Bodies Are Berried

The Lucille Mysteries

Confession Is Murder
Unholy Matrimony
Hit and Nun
A Room with a Pew
Cannoli to Die For

Farmer's Daughter Mysteries

No Farm, No Foul
Sowed to Death
Bought the Farm

The Gourmet De-Lite Mysteries

Allergic to Death
Steamed to Death
Iced to Death

More Books by Peg Cochran

Murder, She Reported Mysteries

Murder, She Reported
Murder, She Uncovered
Murder, She Encountered

Young Adult Books

Oh, Brother!
Truth or Dare

Writing as Meg London

Murder Unmentionable
Laced with Poison
A Fatal Slip

Open Book Mysteries

Murder in the Margins
A Fatal Footnote
Peril on the Page
A Deadly Dedication

Where the Bodies Are Berried

A
CRANBERRY COVE
MYSTERY

Peg Cochran

BEYOND THE PAGE
PUBLISHING

Where the Bodies Are Buried
Peg Cochran
Beyond the Page Books
are published by
Beyond the Page Publishing
www.beyondthepagepub.com

ISBN: 978-1-966322-36-8

Chapter 1

"She kissed you?" Monica said, surprise written all over her face, her eyebrows raised and her mouth open.

"I could tell she was embarrassed about it. She turned bright red and immediately scurried away. I was almost as embarrassed as she was." Greg put the final log in the firepit he and Jeff had dug outside the barn and reached into his pocket for the lighter. He flicked it and held it toward the logs. The kindling caught and flames began to lick the wood. "I tried to dodge her by turning my head but I wasn't quick enough."

Monica turned up the collar of her coat and held her hands out to the fire to warm them. "What possessed her to do that? I know she has a crush on you but still, that's awfully bold for Wilma. When did this happen?"

Wilma was a really useful assistant at Book 'Em, Greg's new and used bookstore in downtown Cranberry Cove, but her habit of following him around with a moony look on her face was driving him a bit crazy.

"About twenty minutes ago." Greg jerked a thumb behind him. "I was in the barn sorting out the lights and suddenly there she was. I hope I didn't inadvertently lead her on in some way."

"I'm sure you didn't." Monica patted his arm. "I wonder where she is now?" Monica put a basket of cranberry muffins on the table that had been set up in front of the firepit. She'd covered it with one of the cranberry-themed tablecloths they'd ordered to sell in the farm store.

"Probably skulking around somewhere." Greg turned to Monica "You're not jealous, are you?"

Monica snorted. "Of course not."

"Not even a little?"

Monica noticed the twinkle in his eye. "Well, maybe a little." She leaned toward her husband and held her face up for a kiss.

Every day she thanked her lucky stars that she and Greg had met. Romance had been the last thing on her mind when she'd moved to Cranberry Cove, but obviously fate had had other ideas.

"There you are." Chelsea Pritchard, the executive director of the

Cranberry Cove Animal Shelter, came jogging over to them. She was panting, her breath sending misty clouds of condensation into the air. Her light brown hair was coming out of its loose bun and her Santa hat was slipping down over her forehead. "Is everything nearly ready?" She twisted her fingers together. "I'm so nervous." She touched Monica's arm. "I can't thank you enough for letting us use your farm for our fundraiser for the animal shelter. We really need the money. We're almost at capacity." She threw her hands in the air. "We even had someone bring in an iguana."

"You should really thank my half brother, Jeff. He owns Sassamanash Farm and has spent a good deal of time clearing out the barn." She gestured toward some large tarp-covered objects. "He had to move all his equipment outside."

Chelsea bit her lower lip. "I hope it's going to be worth it."

Monica squeezed Chelsea's shoulder. She felt her bones poking through her skin under her hand. "I know it's going to be a big success."

Chelsea and Monica had become friends after meeting in a book club Monica had joined when she was pregnant with Teddy. She could hardly believe he was already three months old.

The two of them had put their heads together to come up with the idea for this fundraiser—a chance to have your pet's picture taken with Santa. If she didn't mind saying so herself, Monica thought the idea was pretty brilliant.

Jeff had been happy to allow the animal shelter to use the Sassamanash Farm property for the event. Monica had arrived at the farm on the eastern shore of Lake Michigan during the cranberry harvest several years ago, having fled Chicago when her little café had gone under after the arrival of a chain coffee shop less than a block away. Jeff had needed her help putting the farm back in the black and Monica had agreed, taking over baking for the farm store and keeping the books. It had become an even bigger success than she'd imagined.

By now, the fire crackled and spit loudly, providing welcome warmth on the cold December day. Snow covered the ground with an occasional stubborn weed poking through the crusty top layer and it clung to the trees in the distance, outlining their bare, skeletal branches.

Greg and Jeff had threaded tiny white lights through the bushes alongside the barn, creating a welcome bright spot. Even though it was early in the day, it was more like dusk with the skies obscured by clouds—typical in this part of Michigan, where the proximity of Lake Michigan created what the meteorologist called lake effect clouds as well as lake effect snow.

Monica heard the rumble of a vehicle close by and looked up to see a large truck trundling down the narrow dirt road that led to the barn. It skidded as it headed across the field, its wheels whirring uselessly in the snow. Finally, the tires gripped and it continued its way forward, coming to a stop several feet from the barn. Snow clogged the wheel wells and covered the roof. *Prummel's Props and Events* was written on the side in black script. The driver's door opened and a man jumped down.

He was wearing jeans and a T-shirt but no jacket. Monica shivered just looking at him. "Delivery." He consulted his clipboard. "One Santa sleigh, one Santa throne, two fake Christmas trees, fake snow, two large candy canes, a wooden cutout of an elf and an animal enclosure." He looked up. "Where do you want 'em?"

"It goes in the barn." Monica pointed to the structure. She cleared her throat. "An animal enclosure? What's that for?"

"I don't know, lady. I just deliver the stuff. What you do with it is up to you." He tucked the clipboard under his arm. "Can someone help me unload the stuff? My partner called in sick today and we're short-handed."

"Sure. Let me find someone."

Greg was in the barn and he quickly agreed to lend a hand. Jeff looked over at them and Monica wondered if he had overheard. She hoped she hadn't hurt his feelings by not asking him, but the injury to his arm he had sustained during his tour in Afghanistan would have made it difficult for him.

Monica watched as Greg and the deliveryman brought in the props and slowly turned the very ordinary barn into Santa's North Pole headquarters. The throne was set in the middle of the space flanked by giant candy canes and pine trees frosted with flakes of white. Fake snow, as airy as balls of fluff, completed the effect. Monica imagined viewing it through a child's eyes. It was magical. She couldn't wait until Teddy was old enough to have his picture taken with Santa.

She remembered her mother taking her to Marshall Field's in downtown Chicago to sit on Santa's lap for a picture. She'd worn a red velvet dress with white smocking and black patent-leather Mary Janes, and afterward they'd lunched in the Walnut Room with its forty-five-foot-high Christmas tree glittering with lights displayed in the center.

"I'm going to set up the enclosure. Any particular place?" The deliveryman tapped his clipboard with a pencil.

"Anywhere that seems appropriate."

"Gotcha." He handed her the pencil. "Meanwhile, can you sign for the delivery?"

Chelsea still hadn't appeared so Monica assumed it would be okay for her to sign the receipt. She wished the man a merry Christmas and he saluted as he headed out the door. She couldn't wait for Chelsea to see the incredible transformation of Jeff's barn. Where was she, anyway?

Monica was startled when there was a loud commotion outside. It made her think of the line from "'Twas the Night Before Christmas" — "when out on the roof there arose such a clatter." For one fantastical moment, she envisioned Santa arriving at Sassamanash Farm. She shook herself out of her reverie and went to see what was going on.

A man was leading two live reindeer toward them. Or, perhaps it would be more accurate to say they were leading him. Despite his being built like a barrel with a broad chest, slim waist and wide shoulders, the reindeer were nearly getting the better of him.

"Where do you want these beasts?" he called to Monica.

Once again, she looked around for Chelsea. The arrival of the reindeer had been a surprise, at least to her. Perhaps they were taking the concept of authenticity too far?

She walked over to the fellow. She wrinkled her nose. A strong musky scent surrounded him and the animals.

"I'm Monica Albertson." Monica would have held out her hand but both of his were engaged in grasping the reindeers' reins.

"Jason Vale." He smiled and it transformed his face from rather ordinary into something rather charming.

"Where did they come from?" Monica took a step backward when one of the reindeer suddenly seemed interested in her.

"The North Pole, of course." Vale laughed.

One of the reindeer snorted and Monica looked at it fearfully. "You're not . . . leaving them here, are you?"

"Nah. I'll be here the whole time, don't worry."

Monica spied the wire enclosure the deliveryman had set up. So that's what it was for. "I think they're supposed to go in there."

Vale urged the reindeer into the enclosure and secured it. He kept an eye on them from several paces away as he stuck a cigarette in his mouth and lit it, cupping his hand around the flame of the lighter.

The photographer had arrived and began setting up two enormous lights on stands, moving them a few inches this way and that until he was satisfied. He ran around holding a light meter in his hand and finally, satisfied, centered a tripod in front of Santa's throne.

Monica turned around to see Janice, one of her kitchen staff, heading toward her carrying a large insulated carafe.

"Hot chocolate," she said when she reached Monica. "Where shall I put it? I have a tray with all the fixings too—miniature marshmallows, candy canes, chocolate chips and some whipped cream."

The hot chocolate had been Janice's idea and Monica had been thrilled. She was in favor of anything that helped raise money for the shelter.

"Monica," someone called.

She turned around to see Chelsea bustling toward her with a man in tow. She appeared to be slightly flustered. The man was gray at the temples and gray was sprinkled throughout his dark hair as well. He was wearing a black coat, and a shirt and tie were visible at the open neck.

"This is George Winslow. He's the chairman of the board of commissioners and one of our biggest supporters."

Chelsea's reverent tone made it sound as if she was introducing someone from the royal family.

"Very nice to meet you." Winslow shook Monica's hand. His grip was strong and sure. "My wife loves your cranberry salsa. She orders it every time we go to the Cranberry Cove Inn."

He was a charmer, Monica had to admit. And he all but reeked of money, from his cashmere coat to his silk tie to his fine leather gloves. His name was familiar but she couldn't immediately think why.

The first visitors had begun to arrive—a woman with an elderly chihuahua in a knitted jacket tucked into her tote bag, a husband and wife and two children with a golden doodle who appeared to be delighted by the whole thing, and a young girl with a West Highland white terrier who seemed determined to sniff every single inch of the property.

Shortly afterward, loud and furious barking rang out. A standard poodle had apparently taken offense at the presence of a greyhound and had decided to pick a fight. They snarled and growled at each other while their owners strived valiantly to keep them apart.

Monica groaned. Things weren't getting off to a particularly good start. Maybe this hadn't been such a good idea after all.

Chapter 2

Monica watched as the first person in line approached Santa and tried to cajole her long-haired dachshund to follow her. The dog was far more interested in sniffing the elf cutout and ignored its owner's entreaties. Finally, the woman, who was older and wearing a puffer jacket that made her look twice her size, reached out, grabbed the dog and placed it on Santa's lap, where it immediately began tugging at his beard.

Monica watched in amusement as Santa winced and gently turned the dog around and began to pet it.

So, his beard was real, Monica thought. And he looked as if the padding was all his own too. When the dog was finally still, the photographer snapped the picture, the bright flash startling Monica.

She felt bad that her own rescue dog, Hercule, was back home. Maybe she'd bring him over later to have his picture taken too. Alice was also at the house babysitting Teddy. They'd been so lucky to find her. Teddy was very comfortable with her and rarely cried when Monica left, and when he was napping, Alice even did a few chores around the house. She was a gem, that was for sure.

The dachshund sprinted off, its owner hurrying to catch up, and a man next in line led his pet to Santa. Monica nearly rubbed her eyes in disbelief. The animal at the end of the leash didn't look like a dog unless there was a new breed that looked exactly like a goat. They had called the event Have Your Pet's Picture Taken With Santa. She supposed that offered people enough leeway to define the word *pet*. She shuddered. Hopefully no one had a pet tarantula or snake.

The barn was beginning to feel overly warm from the photographer's bright lights. Monica stepped outside. The frigid air felt wonderful at first but soon she was buttoning her coat and turning up her collar.

She headed over to the refreshment table to check how things were going and to see if they needed more cranberry goodies. She'd spent the last few days baking for this event—cranberry scones, muffins, bread and cookies.

The line for hot chocolate was long. Children gratefully wrapped their hands around the warm cups with marshmallows floating on top and candy canes peeking out the side while their parents handed over dollar bills.

"Need any help? You have quite a crowd forming," Monica asked the woman manning the carafe. "I'm Monica Albertson, by the way."

The cold had pinched the tip of the woman's rather bulbous nose with red. In contrast to her nose, her face was narrow and the skin drooped from her sharp cheekbones.

"Sharon Dort," she answered. She nodded her head toward the line behind her. "We're doing a brisk business." She smiled. "All the more money for the animal shelter."

"Are you a volunteer there?"

"Yes. I walk the dogs, help keep the place clean. I'm a whiz with a broom. Dust bunnies can't hide from me. Whatever needs done, I'll do it." She paused. "It's hard sometimes. I love all the animals and wish I could find them all homes."

"Monica!"

"Excuse me." Monica touched Sharon on the arm lightly and looked around for whoever it was who had called her name. She saw Janice beckoning her and hurried over.

Janice wore her customary dour expression. Monica knew that behind that rigid exterior was a very kind person.

"What is it?"

Janice gestured toward the firepit. "We need a couple more logs for the fire. I'd get them myself but my lumbago is acting up." She shook her head. "Look at that."

Monica swiveled around. She didn't see anything out of the ordinary. "Look at what?"

"That cat sitting with its back to the fire."

Monica looked and a cat on a leash was indeed sitting with its back to the fire.

"You know what that means, don't you?"

Monica now knew what it meant when people said they felt *at sea.*

"A storm's coming." Janice said it as surely as if she'd seen evidence of it on radar. She pointed at the sky. "See?"

Monica dutifully looked up but all she saw was the same dark clouds that had been hovering over them all day.

Fire had burned through one of the logs in the firepit and it popped loudly and split in two.

"Better get that seen to."

"I'll find Greg and have him get some more wood."

She found Greg chatting with Jeff near the equipment Jeff had removed from the barn. They each had a travel mug of coffee in hand, and judging by the crumbs trailing down the front of their jackets, they had enjoyed some baked goods as well.

"Greg," Monica called, "we need some more wood for the fire."

"Sure thing." He handed his travel mug to Monica and she inhaled the enticing scent of freshly brewed coffee. She hoped Greg wouldn't mind if she took a sip.

"Be careful." Jeff wiped his mouth with the back of his hand. "There's a spider's nest in the wood pile somewhere. I got bitten the other day." He pulled up his sleeve. There was an inflamed red bump just above his wrist.

Monica frowned. "Do you think you should have that looked at?"

Jeff waved a hand. "Nah. It's fine. It just itches. But I promise if it gets any worse I'll see a doctor."

"I'll be careful. I have no desire to be bitten by a spider." Greg headed toward the side of the barn where the logs were neatly stacked.

Monica took a sip of Greg's coffee and sighed. The warmth felt so good. Even though she'd piled on multiple layers—thermal shirt, long-sleeved T-shirt, sweater and puffer jacket—she still felt the cold. She missed the days when she was pregnant with Teddy and no matter how chilly it was, she always felt as if she was standing in front of a blast furnace.

George Winslow was over by the reindeer enclosure and appeared to be studying the scene. Monica wondered whether she should go and talk to him. He was a large donor to the Cranberry Cove Animal Shelter, after all, and was an honored guest at the event. Before she could move, a woman approached him and they began a conversation.

At first, the woman appeared to be expensively dressed, but on second glance, Monica realized her Louis Vuitton handbag and Gucci shoes were knockoffs. She'd seen enough of the real thing when she worked in Chicago to know the difference. Not that it mattered to her. To each his own was her motto. She was more comfortable in her worn jeans and corduroys and favorite sweaters and didn't hanker after designer clothing. Which was a good thing, because with a new baby and a new house she certainly couldn't afford to buy any.

The woman was gesturing a lot while Winslow kept his hands shoved in his coat pockets. The more frantic the woman's gestures became, the more bemused Winslow looked. The woman's Yorkie sniffed the man's shoes and then, obviously bored, curled up at its owner's feet and closed its eyes.

The woman's voice got louder and it was clear they were having an argument. Although the woman was doing all the arguing. Winslow didn't appear to be saying much of anything. He was regarding his female companion the way one would a pesky fly—a nuisance but nothing to be concerned about.

Monica shook herself. It was none of her business and it was time she made herself useful. She began to turn away, and as she did, she noticed Winslow's irate companion had given up and was walking toward the line of waiting pets and their owners.

Winslow turned on his heel and headed toward the refreshment stand, when another woman joined him. She linked her arm through his and smiled up at him. His expression didn't change. This woman appeared to be in her forties and was well-dressed in a country club sort of way—polished ankle boots, gray flannel slacks, a shearling jacket and a cream-colored scarf at her neck. Cashmere? Monica wondered.

Monica moved closer to the fire. Greg had put on several more logs and they were burning brightly. Heavier clouds had moved in and the temperature had dropped even further. She glanced at her watch. They would be closing down soon.

Jason Vale was showing two children in matching parkas how to feed the reindeer treats. They were so bundled up, Monica couldn't tell if they were boys or girls or one of each.

Greg appeared with Hercule in tow. A couple of years ago, Hercule had wandered into Book 'Em looking thin and disheveled. Unable to locate his owner, Greg and Monica had adopted him. Now, Monica couldn't imagine their little family without him.

"You need a trip to the groomer," Monica said, brushing some of the fur out of Hercule's eyes. She could have sworn he gave her the side-eye at that.

Hercule appeared to be thrilled with Santa, wagging his tail, his ears back and his bright pink tongue lolling out. He was a bit large for Santa's lap, but Monica managed to turn him around to face the camera for the shot.

"I'll ask Wilma to run him home," Greg said, taking hold of Hercule's leash. He looked around. "Where is she, by the way?"

"I haven't seen her in ages. Perhaps she's taking a break. Meanwhile, I have to find Chelsea."

There were no more pets and owners in line to see Santa and Santa was standing next to his red and gold velvet chair, stretching his arms overhead.

Finally, everyone had left, their pets in tow. Monica was relieved that the only out-of-the-ordinary animal that had come to be photographed with Santa was the goat, and it had been very well-behaved. Certainly better behaved than the Jack Russell terrier who had slipped its collar and had tried to run off with a cranberry scone it snatched from someone's hand.

Vale was leashing up the reindeer and Sharon was collecting the unused cups and napkins. Greg and Jeff were busy putting out the fire in the firepit, while Chelsea was nowhere to be seen. Monica was beginning to worry about her when she suddenly appeared.

She was breathless and slightly disheveled. "Sorry to take off like that. One of the owners was having trouble getting her Great Dane into the car. It has arthritis, poor thing. Together we managed to get it inside and situated comfortably."

A rumble in the distance announced the arrival of the truck from Prummel's Props and Events. This time the driver had a helper with him and they made short work of clearing all the props out of the barn.

Monica grabbed a garbage bag from the stash next to the refreshment table and began picking up trash. There wasn't much, mostly wrappers from the candy canes and a handful of discarded foam cups. The snow, which had been pristine and white, was now trampled with footprints and streaked with mud.

Monica bent to pick up a dollar bill that must have fallen out of someone's pocket, but a gust of wind caught it and sent it cartwheeling across the snow. Monica scampered after it, but as soon as she got close, the wind caught it and sent it whirling again. It was as if the wind was playing a game with her, Monica thought. A game she didn't appreciate one bit. Her toes were becoming numb and the tips of her fingers ached with cold.

The wandering dollar bill led her around to the side of the barn, where it settled next to a mound of snow.

"Finally," Monica muttered under her breath as she bent to pick it up.

She was straightening up when she noticed something peculiar. Something red had stained the top of the heap of snow. As she eyed it, additional red began seeping through the snow.

What on earth?

Monica knelt next to the mound, which was long but not very high. With her gloved hands, she began to brush the snow away. As she did, the snow became redder and redder until suddenly she was staring into the face of George Winslow, who appeared to be quite dead. Quite dead, indeed.

Chapter 3

Monica didn't even realize she was screaming until Greg and Jeff came tearing around the side of the barn. They slid to a halt at the mound of snow partially covering Winslow's body.

Monica was shivering and her teeth were chattering. Greg put his arms around her and she buried her face against his chest.

"What on earth?" Jeff had turned pale. "Who is it?"

Monica lifted her head. "It's George Winslow. He is . . . was one of the animal shelter's biggest donors."

Greg pulled his phone from his pocket and whipped off his gloves. "I'm calling the police." He looked at Monica. "Are you okay?"

"I'm fine." Monica took a deep breath and blew it out, trying to relax her shoulders. This wasn't the first time she'd encountered a dead body, but the sight still unnerved her and she hoped she'd never become so jaded that it didn't.

Greg had a brief conversation with the police dispatcher then pocketed his phone. "They're on their way." He put his gloves back on.

Lazy snowflakes began to drift down from the sky and Monica began to shiver again.

"Sis, why don't you wait in the barn? It's a bit warmer in there. Greg and I will handle this."

It was a very tempting offer. "The police will want to talk to me since I found the body."

Jeff tilted his head toward the dirt path leading to the farm. "You'll hear them coming, don't worry."

The wind had picked up and the snow was falling faster. Flakes dotted Jeff's knit cap and the shoulders of Greg's jacket.

The barn was slightly warmer than outdoors and Monica was grateful for the shelter. She hoped the police would hurry. Greg and Jeff must be freezing standing out in the open.

Jeff was right. Monica clearly heard the sirens in the distance as the police raced toward the farm. She looked out the door and saw two patrol cars rattling down the dirt path.

She was reluctant to leave the relative warmth of the barn but she stepped outside when she heard the officers' brakes squeal to a stop.

Icy snow flakes stung her face and clung to her hair as she reluctantly joined Greg and Jeff.

A larger patch of snow was stained red now. Monica averted her eyes, instead watching as two police officers made their way toward them. She was surprised to see that one of them was female. She was tiny and looked weighted down by the equipment hanging from her belt. The microphone on her shoulder crackled as she approached them.

"Detective Stevens has been notified," she said. "We'll get the scene roped off."

Snow was falling in earnest now. "If you want to wait in the barn?" She cocked her head in that direction.

Monica didn't need a second invitation, but before she got to the shelter of the barn, a car pulled up in back of the patrol car and Stevens got out.

Her short blond bob was tucked behind her ears and she had a knitted cap pulled down over her forehead. She was nearly swallowed up by her fur-trimmed parka and her hands were stuffed in her pockets.

She nodded at Monica, Greg and Jeff and stood staring at Winslow's body for several minutes. "Do we know who it is?" She turned to Monica. "He looks familiar."

"George Winslow. He's the county commissioner."

"No wonder. I've met him before." She rolled her eyes. "He was quite impressed with himself. He made a fortune with his pharmaceutical company, WinGeo Pharmaceuticals." She walked around the body. "Do we know how he got here?" She raised her eyebrows and they disappeared under the brim of her cap.

Monica explained about the fundraising event. "We called it 'have your pet's picture taken with Santa.'"

"Seriously?" Stevens's expression was quizzical. "Animals having their picture taken with Santa? I've seen clothing for pets, Halloween costumes, gourmet food and treats, but this is a new one. What will they think of next."

By now, the area had been encircled with crime scene tape and the two officers stood to the side awaiting orders.

Stevens crouched down next to the body. "It looks as if he was bashed over the head. That must be where the blood is coming from.

But we won't know for sure until the medical examiner confirms it. With any luck, he'll also be able to give us some idea of what the murder weapon might have been."

She straightened up and Monica heard her back crack. She looked around, dismay on her face. "We won't get anything from all these footprints.

Stevens bent down again and spent several minutes studying the body. "Wait," she said suddenly. "What's this?" She brushed a bit more snow away.

Nestled in the snow was a glass bottle. Monica thought it looked like the bottles cough syrup came in. Bits of the label still stuck to it, but the majority of it had been stripped off.

Stevens yanked off her wool gloves and fished a pair of blue vinyl ones from her pocket along with a plastic evidence bag. She pulled the gloves on and reached for the bottle.

It caught the light as she turned it this way and that, examining it, before dropping it into the evidence bag.

"Do you think that has something to do with the murder?" Monica pulled her hat lower over her ears.

Stevens's mouth quirked to one side. "Who knows? It might. Then again it could be a coincidence — the sort that sends us on a useless wild-goose chase."

Chapter 4

"I think I have a murder hangover." Monica pushed her plate away and rubbed her forehead. She picked up a tiny piece of bacon and handed it to Hercule, who gobbled it down happily. "If there is such a thing."

She offered a piece to Mittens, but Mittens turned up her nose at it and retreated to the corner, where she began to groom herself.

Greg stabbed the last piece of pancake on his plate and paused with his fork in the air. "I wouldn't be surprised if there was such a thing, although I doubt you'll find it on WebMD. Yesterday was . . . grueling. Such a grim ending to such a festive day."

Monica leaned her elbows on the table. "I'm still processing what happened. I keep hoping Stevens will call and say it was simply an unfortunate accident."

"Sadly, I doubt that. It's possible Winslow could have tripped, fallen and banged his head on something, but he couldn't have covered himself up with snow. Whoever did it didn't want him to be found. At least not right away." Greg nibbled on his last piece of bacon.

"And that medicine bottle. At least I think that's what it was."

"Someone could have dropped it there when they were here for the bog tours in the fall." Greg wiped his lips with his napkin and tossed it on the table.

"True, but I can't shake the feeling it has something to do with Winslow's death."

Monica got up and took their empty plates to the counter. Sun streamed in the large window over the sink and once again Monica marveled that this house was really theirs. She'd loved their little cottage on the farm, but with a new baby she relished having more space.

She rinsed the dishes and handed them to Greg, who stacked them in the dishwasher. They were almost done when the doorbell rang.

"I'm not expecting anyone, are you?" Monica pulled off her rubber gloves.

Greg shook his head. "I'll get it."

Monica grinned. "Protecting me from possible intruders?"

"Of course," he said as he headed toward the door.

He opened the door and Chelsea nearly stumbled over the sill. "I hope I'm not disturbing you."

"Not at all. Please come in." Greg stood aside and Chelsea walked into the kitchen.

She stood there staring like a deer caught in the headlights of an oncoming car. She was wearing jeans that were too big, as if she'd lost weight, and a heavy fisherman's knit sweater. Her hands were pulled up inside the sleeves as if they were cold.

"Let's go sit down." Monica picked up the baby monitor from the kitchen table and led the way into the adjoining family room.

A dark blue sectional sofa took up most of the space. Monica had looked longingly at the cream-colored ones in the store but had opted for practicality instead. Teddy would soon be toddling around, no doubt with sticky hands, and the sofa wouldn't have stayed so beautifully pristine for long. She put the baby monitor on the coffee table and took a seat. When she looked over at Chelsea, she saw she was shaking slightly and her face looked pinched, as if she hadn't slept well.

"What's wrong?" As soon as she said it, Monica realized that it was a stupid thing to say. Winslow's murder must have stunned Chelsea as much as it had, her even if she hadn't found the body herself.

Chelsea was about to answer when a cry came through the baby monitor.

"Sounds like Teddy's awake. I'll get him." Greg got up and went toward the stairs.

Chelsea was silent, sitting diagonally across from Monica and picking at her cuticles, which were already red and raw-looking.

"I saw the news last night. About . . . about Mr. Winslow's death. They said they suspect murder. How could that be?"

"We won't know for sure until the investigation is complete. It's probably best not to jump to conclusions." Monica thought of Winslow's body lying on the ground with blood seeping through the snow and had to suppress a shudder.

There was a long silence. "The police want to talk to me," Chelsea finally blurted out.

So that was what was upsetting her, Monica thought. "It's just standard operating procedure in a murder investigation. Detective Stevens will be talking to everyone at some point, including me."

"She said she was coming to my place. I didn't know what to do so I put my coat on right away and came here."

"You mean you left before she got to your house . . . ?"

Chelsea rubbed her hands on her thighs. "Yes. I know I shouldn't have done that but I panicked."

"You really don't have anything to worry about." Monica hoped her words would put Chelsea at ease, but Chelsea continued to pick at a loose thread on her sweater. "It doesn't mean they think you had anything to do with Winslow's death. Why on earth would you murder George Winslow?"

"I didn't murder him. You have to believe me. But I don't think the police will."

"But why? What could your motive have possibly been?"

"The shelter is in trouble. We need money," Chelsea mumbled half under her breath.

"But why would that—?"

Chelsea scrubbed her hands over her face. "I knew . . . I knew Winslow had left the shelter a large portion of his estate." She looked at Monica. "Now do you see why I'm worried?"

"I don't think—"

Chelsea reached out and grabbed Monica's hands. "You've got to help me. I know you've done this before. You have to find out who really killed Mr. Winslow."

Chapter 5

Monica was peeling potatoes for a pot roast for their dinner when the front doorbell rang. She put down the peeler, wiped her hands on her apron and went to answer it.

"I hope I'm not interrupting anything," Stevens said as she wiped her feet on the doormat. She was wearing tan corduroy pants and her coat was open, revealing a bright blue turtleneck sweater.

"Come in." Monica swept the door open wider.

Stevens paused to take off her boots and then stood for a moment eyeing Monica's family room and kitchen.

"This is lovely. You and Greg must be thrilled."

"We are." Monica was about to sit down but changed her mind. "Can I get you anything? Tea? Coffee?"

"Make it a martini and you have a deal." Stevens laughed and kneaded her forehead.

"Rough day?"

"Rough couple of weeks. Two auto break-ins, and unfortunately both cars were BMWs and belonged to tourists, a rock thrown through someone's window, a hit-and-run. Fortunately, the pedestrian only suffered minor injuries. Oh, and an attempted arson by a couple of teenagers with too much time on their hands."

She ran her hands through her hair. "And it's almost Christmas. Only a few more weeks to go." She gestured toward the corner of the room. "At least you've got your tree up."

Monica looked around. She was proud of what she'd done with the room—the tree, of course, but also a garland with tiny white lights on the mantel and wreaths in each of the windows.

"I don't suppose you have to agonize over what to get Teddy since he's still a baby."

"What is your son asking Santa for?"

"One of those video game players. I've got the name written down somewhere. I suppose I'll have to find the time to drive to Grand Rapids and one of those big box stores." She smiled. "But this must be exciting for you. Teddy's first Christmas."

Monica felt sheepish. "I have to admit I've already bought a My First Christmas bib, an ornament for the tree and a long-sleeved onesie."

Stevens cleared her throat and slapped her thighs. "I suppose I should tell you why I'm here."

Monica's expression turned somber. "I think I can guess."

"The medical examiner has confirmed that Winslow was hit over the head with something. He was quite positive he didn't fall and hit his head, which makes this murder. He's doing the autopsy tomorrow and will have more information for us about the possible murder weapon."

Stevens leaned back and crossed her legs. "I'm hoping you can help me. I understand the event was a fundraiser for our local animal shelter. I wanted to talk to the director of the shelter but she seems to be avoiding me." Her tone was sarcastic. "I'll catch up with her eventually."

Why had Chelsea been so foolish, Monica wondered. She'd only made it worse for herself.

"Of course, this had to happen at an event with hordes of people. Nothing is ever simple, is it?" She sighed. "I need some help. Did you notice anything . . . unusual at yesterday's event?"

Monica tried to think back. She didn't suppose Stevens was interested in hearing about the goat. "I can't think of anything in particular. Everything went quite smoothly."

"Why was Winslow there? Did he bring a pet?"

"No. But he is involved with the shelter thanks to his role as county commissioner. I suppose that's why he decided to attend."

"Did he interact with anyone?"

"Well, with Chelsea obviously. She introduced him to me." Monica squeezed her eyebrows together. An image came into view. "Oh," she exclaimed, nearly startling Stevens. "Most of the time, Winslow was off standing by himself observing everything. But then a woman went up to him. At first, they were talking, but then it became clear they were arguing."

Stevens frowned. "How did Winslow react?"

"He didn't. The whole thing looked as if it amused him."

"I don't suppose you recognized the woman?"

"I'm sorry, no."

"Would anyone else possibly know? Did someone else see her?"

"I don't know." Monica gave an apologetic smile. "But there was someone else, too. Another woman went up to him and hooked her arm through his. I assumed it was his wife."

Stevens slapped her knee. "Great. I was planning to talk to Mrs. Winslow next. Perhaps she will have an idea of who that other woman was."

• • •

Monica was in the kitchen checking on the pot roast when Greg turned on the television in the family room. The familiar WZZZ news jingle came on. Monica was setting the table when she heard Sassamanash Farm mentioned and whirled around.

"Come see this," Greg beckoned to her. "It's about Winslow's murder."

Monica hastened into the family room and plopped on the couch next to Greg. Teddy was in his carry cot fast asleep, his long eyelashes casting shadows on his round cheeks. Monica felt the familiar catch in her breath that happened every time she looked at him. She couldn't imagine loving anything more.

Hercule was next to the carry cot, his eyebrows waggling up and down as if checking for danger, and Mittens was curled up on the other end of the sofa.

A reporter was standing in a high school gym in front of a stand with a trophy on it and a basketball team lined up in the background. "And now over to you, Jack."

"Thanks, Karla."

The camera switched to the WZZZ news anchor, who was seated behind his desk with a somber expression on his face. A picture of George Winslow was on a screen in the background.

"We have some sad news for you. George Winslow, founder and CEO of WinGeo Pharmaceuticals, has died. The police are investigating his alleged murder yesterday at a fundraiser for his favorite charity, the Cranberry Cove Animal Shelter. Winslow started WinGeo Pharmaceuticals more than two decades ago, and under his skilled leadership it grew to be the success it is today."

He cleared his throat. "Winslow was born in Cranberry Cove and attended Michigan State University, graduating with a degree in chemistry. He holds several patents and has received numerous awards for his work in the pharmaceutical field. He is survived by his widow, Debra." A picture of Debra flashed on the screen.

Monica pointed at the television. "That's the woman I saw him with at the fundraiser. So, she's his wife. I thought so."

"His first marriage to the former Angela DeBoer ended in divorce," the anchor continued. "The police will release further details as they become available."

"Isn't the spouse always the first suspect?" Greg reached down and scratched the top of Hercule's head.

"Yes. And that's why I think I'd like to find out more about Mrs. George Winslow."

Chapter 6

Monica had just finished feeding Teddy Monday morning when the doorbell rang.

"Yoo-hoo!" Alice called out. "I'm here. Where's that precious boy?"

"We're in the kitchen." Monica pulled the burp cloth off her shoulder and put it on the counter.

"It feels like snow out there." Alice took off her jacket and hung it from the coat tree by the back door. Her face was red and Monica felt waves of cold coming off her.

"How's our boy today?" She held her hands out for Teddy.

Once again, Monica thanked heaven that she'd found Alice. She'd been a nurse and had raised a number of children of her own, and Monica never had any worries when Teddy was with her.

Monica glanced at the kitchen clock. "I should get going. There's a lot to do today." She grabbed her jacket from the coat tree, slipped it on, wound her scarf around her neck and pulled her gloves out of her pocket.

She kissed Teddy on the cheek and ran her hand over his downy head. She always felt a pang when she left him but he was in good hands.

A thin blanket of snow had fallen overnight, making everything look pristine again—footprints filled in, the blackened snow alongside the road white again.

The drive to the farm didn't take long. She and Greg had been lucky to find a piece of land for their house that was halfway between the farm and the bookstore.

The farm kitchen was humming when Monica arrived. Mick was pulling a sheet of muffins from the oven, Janice was kneading a lump of dough, slapping it down on the counter then picking it up again, and Nancy, Monica's mother, was piping icing on a tray of scones, a look of concentration on her face and the tip of her tongue caught between her teeth.

"The Cranberry Cove Inn called." Mick flung his oven mitts on the counter. "They want two dozen jars of compote as soon as possible. That is good news, right?" He gave the smile that, along with his Greek god good looks, had captivated everyone.

"I'd better get to work then." Monica hung up her jacket and pulled on a pair of nylon food safety gloves.

There was a stack of crates in the corner stamped with *Sassamanash Farm* and filled with fresh cranberries. Monica went to pick one up but Mick stopped her.

"That's heavy. Let me do it for you." He lifted the crate as if it was weightless and carried it over to the counter. Monica had put a large strainer in the sink and Mick dumped in the cranberries.

She ran water over them then transferred them to a large pot she'd set out on the burner. She grabbed the carton of sugar and peered into it. It was nearly empty. She grabbed another from the storeroom, measured out the correct amount and added it to the pot, along with some orange zest, orange juice and a dash of vanilla to round out the flavors.

"You're awfully quiet today." Monica turned to look at Mick. "Is there something on your mind?"

He ran his hands over his face. "My father called last night from Greece. I knew right away it wasn't good. He always worries about the cost of calling long distance and wouldn't do it if it wasn't something urgent."

"Is everything okay?"

Mick heaved a sigh. "My mother has to have surgery. My father said the doctor assured him it was quite routine, but I don't know. I'm afraid there's something he's not telling me." He waved a hand around the kitchen. His voice caught in his throat. "And I can't even be there."

Monica patted his arm. "I'm sure your father would tell you if it was serious."

Mick grunted and picked up the rolling pin.

The cranberries in the pot on the stove began to bubble, pop and spit as they broke down into a delicious compote.

"How did your event go?" Nancy began putting the finished scones into a box to deliver to the farm store.

"You didn't hear?" Janice stood with her hands on her hips.

Nancy looked confused. "No. What happened?"

Monica explained about finding Winslow's body.

Nancy's mouth hung open. "How awful. I play bridge with his wife, Debra. She must be devastated. I'll have to give her a call."

Monica's ears perked up. "You know Mrs. Winslow?"

"Yes. Not well. Just socially."

"Does she talk about her husband at all?"

Nancy frowned. "I know she's his second wife but they've been married for years. I don't recall her complaining, although the last few times we played, she did seem a bit . . . out of sorts. She said she'd scheduled an eyelid lift with a plastic surgeon in Grand Rapids and I thought perhaps she was worried about the upcoming surgery."

"Is she feeling insecure about her looks?" Monica stirred the pot of compote. It was nearly done.

"Oh, pooh," Janice said. "A man doesn't care about a woman's looks after he marries her. All he wants is a clean house, clean clothes and a hot dinner on the table every night."

"That didn't work out too well for me." Nancy gave a half smile. "I did all of those things and it wasn't enough."

"That wasn't about you, Mom. It was more about Dad than anything." Monica stirred the compote. "Do you think Mrs. Winslow is worried about her marriage?"

"I don't know. She hasn't mentioned it."

"Men with money like Winslow get restless," Janice said with finality. "They like to show off and having a trophy wife on their arm is part of it. That is what they call it, isn't it?"

Monica decided to end the conversation. "We have to get this compote bottled up so I can deliver it to the Inn."

Everyone quieted down and got back to work.

• • •

With the jars of compote loaded into her trunk, Monica headed toward downtown Cranberry Cove. She shivered when Lake Michigan came into view. The water was gray with fingers of ice reaching out into the lake.

Downtown Cranberry Cove looked considerably more hospitable, with wreaths hanging from each of the old-fashioned gas lights and on the doors of the shops and garlands wound around the lampposts. The Van Velsens, identical twin owners of Gumdrops, Cranberry Cove's candy store, had a small tree decorated with lights and brightly colored ornaments in a ceramic pot outside their door.

Monica drove down to the Inn, where the large pine tree out front had been strung with white lights and silver beads. She pulled into the driveway and around the back to the service entrance. Within minutes the door opened and a young man came out. The sleeves of his sweatshirt were rolled up and he had a dark blue baseball cap on backward.

"Whatcha got for me?" he said as Monica opened her trunk.

"A carton of compote. The chef is waiting for it."

The fellow pointed at the label on one of the jars. "Sassamanash Farm. Isn't that where that murder took place?" His expression was eager.

Monica didn't want to get into a conversation about Winslow's death. "Yes," she said as she went around the car and opened her door. "Listen, I've got to go."

The fellow shrugged. "Sure."

Goodness. Was everyone going to associate murder with Sassamanash Farm? It wasn't the first time someone had been killed there but over time, people had forgotten about it. Was she going to be bombarded with questions every time she went out?

As Monica headed away from the Inn, she had a sudden impulse. She'd stop in and see Greg. He'd left early and she'd missed him that morning.

She pulled into a parking space nearby and got out. The wind coming off the lake was frigid and it immediately snatched her scarf and blew it across her face. The blast of warm air when she opened the door to Book 'Em felt heavenly.

Greg was behind the counter and a checkout line had formed. His dark hair was a bit disheveled and he looked slightly panic-stricken.

Where was Wilma? Monica glanced around the store but didn't immediately see her. She must be in the stockroom or perhaps she's taken a break for lunch.

Greg looked at her over the counter and smiled apologetically. Monica made a *don't worry about it* motion and went to peruse the books on the display table.

She picked up a book here and there, read the blurb on the back and returned it to the display. She was so busy between the farm kitchen and taking care of Teddy that she had barely any time to read. She had to remedy that. Reading was important and a wonderful way to relax. Watching the news had become quite stressful and she and Greg hadn't signed up for any of the streaming platforms everyone else seemed to have.

By the time she'd selected a book, Greg had taken care of all of his customers.

"You're busy this morning," Monica said as she pecked him on the lips. "Where's Wilma? Out to lunch?"

Greg ran his hands through his hair, leaving it even more disheveled. "She didn't show up today. I tried calling her but she didn't answer her phone."

"That's not like Wilma at all."

"It certainly isn't." Greg stuffed his hands in his pockets. "She's usually here before I am with the coffee already brewing."

"Do you think it has anything to do with what happened on Saturday?"

"Certainly, she'd have gotten over any embarrassment by now." Greg straightened a book display on the counter.

"I hope she's okay. Do you think we should check on her? Maybe she's sick?"

Greg frowned. "She's even shown up when she was sick. I've had to send her home before she passed it on to everyone else."

Monica's hand flew to her mouth. She shook her head. "No, it's not possible. Not Wilma."

"What?"

Monica looked up at him. "It just occurred to me. What if she had something to do with Winslow's murder?"

• • •

Monica thought about it on her drive back to the farm. It was impossible to imagine Wilma as a murderer, but there had been highly unlikely killers before. She tried to think of what she knew about Wilma and came up empty-handed. Wilma had always just . . . been there. She felt a wave of guilt. She should have made more of an effort to get to know her.

She was almost to the farm when her cell phone rang. She debated answering it. But what if it was Alice and something was wrong with Teddy? The thought sent her heart pounding hard against her chest and her breath coming in gasps. She pulled over to the side of the road and fished her cell phone out of her purse.

She recognized the number and her heart beat and breathing slowed. It was Chelsea. Was she going to react like this every time the phone rang? Her fingers were still shaking a bit as she hit the answer key and said hello.

"Monica, this is Chelsea." She sounded as distressed as Monica had felt moments ago.

"What's up? Is something wrong?"

Chelsea sniffed. "Can you come here? I'll make us a coffee and I have some freshly baked cookies that Sharon made."

Monica debated. There was still work to do but she had managed to get the compote delivered. She supposed she could spare some time.

"Sure. I'll be there shortly."

She'd already passed the street for the animal shelter and pulled into someone's driveway to turn around. Within minutes, she was heading down the bumpy driveway in front of the Cranberry Cove Animal Shelter. It was a long, low building encircled by a chain link fence. She heard dogs barking as she got out of her car and made her way to the door.

Chelsea was waiting for her. Her face was pinched with worry and her hair was yanked back into a ponytail with strands hanging limply around her face.

"We can sit in my office." She led Monica down the hall, where the barking grew louder. "That's our Maltese-Chihuahua mix. Precious. Her bark is bigger than she is."

Chelsea's office was bare bones with a metal desk, file cabinets and a chair for visitors that Monica discovered rocked slightly when she sat down. Chelsea's chair had black electrical tape mending gashes in the fabric on the arms and the seat was sagging. The walls were cinder block and the room was windowless.

"Not very luxurious, I know." Chelsea plopped into the chair behind the desk. "We try to make sure as much money as possible goes toward the animals."

Monica braced her feet on the floor to stop her chair from wobbling. "What did you want to talk to me about? You sounded upset."

Chelsea swiveled her chair back and forth. It groaned each time she moved. "I suppose it's rather silly really but they seem to be taking it very seriously."

"What is? Who is?"

"The Bischoffs and the Jonkers. They're all up in arms about it."

Thoughts raced through Monica's mind but she couldn't imagine what Chelsea was talking about.

Chelsea laid her hands down flat on the desk. "The Bischoffs claim that the Jonkers' beagle got their golden doodle pregnant at the event at your farm on Saturday."

"What does that have to do with you? You could hardly have prevented it."

"I know." Chelsea kneaded her knuckles. "But they're threatening to sue and we can't afford a lawyer." She put her elbows on her desk and her chin on her hands. "I talked to Diana, she volunteers here sometimes and is in her third year of law school, and she said she doubted they had a leg to stand on, let alone four." She laughed.

"I don't know anything about the law but I'd have to agree with Diana. I don't see how they can blame you for that."

"I'm sure you're right. But it's one more thing to worry about and one more thing to deal with. My plate is already full enough as it is." She groaned. "All this on top of George Winslow's death." Her hand jerked and it bumped some rolled-up sheets of paper that had been on the edge of her desk.

They unfurled slightly as they rolled across the floor. Monica bent to pick them up. She was about to hand them to Chelsea when she paused. The papers looked like architectural drawings. They reminded her of the ones the architect had drawn up for the house she and Greg had had built.

She knew Chelsea lived in a small house on one of the streets behind St. Andrews Church. Were these plans for her?

"Are you adding on to your house?" Monica put the roll of papers on Chelsea's desk.

Chelsea's face paled, then a flush rose up her neck and slowly crept to her forehead. She fidgeted with some papers on the desk and didn't look at Monica.

"Not exactly," she mumbled.

Monica waited. Chelsea continued to stare down at her hands.

Her head jerked up.

"The plans are for the shelter. For an addition. It's pie in the sky really. The shelter doesn't have the money but someday . . ." She shrugged.

Monica nodded. She didn't know what to say, although she knew what she was thinking. Winslow's death was quite fortuitous. Chelsea knew he was leaving a good portion of his estate to the shelter. She wanted to expand and had even had plans drawn up, as if she knew the money was going to appear.

The shelter meant everything to Chelsea. She wasn't married, had no children, and as far as Monica could tell, didn't even have a boyfriend. She'd do anything for the shelter.

Maybe even commit murder.

Chapter 7

Monica worked extra hard all afternoon to make up for her absence. She felt guilty about having stopped in to see Chelsea, although Mick had assured her that everything was going just fine. She pulled her second batch of cranberry-banana loaves from the oven and the aroma wafting from them reminded her that she hadn't had anything to eat since breakfast.

She grabbed one of the yogurts she kept stashed in the refrigerator, gulped it down and went back to work.

"Phew." Mick ran his forearm across his forehead, which was shiny with sweat from the heat of the oven. "I think that's enough for today." He yanked off his apron.

Monica looked at the clock and was surprised to see the time. "I think you're right. Janice took a load of goods down to the farm store. They should be okay for now."

Nancy sighed. "I'm in no hurry. I'm paying a condolence call on Debra Winslow and I'm not looking forward to it. What do you say to a woman whose husband didn't just die but was murdered?"

"I'll go with you," Monica blurted out.

"Would you, dear? That would make it so much easier. We won't stay long. Debra's probably not up for a long visit anyway. People have probably been coming and going all day."

"We should take something. I'll pack up a loaf of cranberry bread for her."

"I'll get it for you." Mick deftly wrapped up a loaf of cranberry bread and handed it to Monica. It was still warm.

"Let's take my car," Nancy said. "It's more comfortable."

Just then the door opened and Gina, Monica's stepmother, breezed in. Living in Cranberry Cove hadn't put much of a dent in her rather eclectic style. She was wearing leopard-print leggings, black suede boots and a leather moto jacket.

Nancy looked her up and down and raised an eyebrow, disapproval written on her face.

The two Mrs. Albertsons couldn't have been more different. Monica often wondered what had possessed her father to ping-pong from one to the other. Life with Monica's mother had been structured and sedate, while life with Gina had been considerably more chaotic.

"Are you leaving?" Gina looked from Monica to Nancy.

Nancy made a sad face. "We're paying a condolence call on Debra Winslow."

Gina's eyebrows shot up. "Debra Winslow? Why? Who died?"

Nancy cleared her throat. "Her husband, George."

"That's terrible."

Monica was surprised Gina hadn't already learned about the murder. She normally had her ear to the ground and could be counted on to hear the beating of the drums before anyone else.

"Micky and I managed to get away for a bit to this little inn up north. It was very romantic." She fluttered her eyelashes. "Why don't I go with you?"

Both Monica and Nancy stared at her. Nancy raised her eyebrows. "Do you know Debra Winslow?"

"She comes into my store frequently. We always have a bit of a chat."

"You mean you're trading gossip." Nancy reached for her coat. "Debra does love to spread news around. She's always the first to know about something and the last to stop talking about it."

Nancy opened the door and a gust of wind blew across the transom. "We're taking my car. It's more comfortable. Besides, we don't want to look like a convoy descending on her in three separate cars."

Monica let Gina sit up front. Nancy got behind the wheel, hands at two and ten o'clock, and started the car. It jounced down the dirt road and Monica was relieved when they reached the main thoroughfare.

Nancy looked right, left and right again before turning. Monica could sense Gina's impatience from the set of her shoulders and the rapidity of her breathing.

"The speed limit is forty-five. You can go faster, you know. We're barely doing thirty-five." Gina drove as if speed limits were mere suggestions.

Nancy ignored her. Finally, they approached the one stoplight before entering downtown Cranberry Cove.

"Step on it," Gina yelled. "The light's yellow. We can make it."

Nancy ignored her, put her foot on the brake and they slowed to a stop.

Gina and Nancy continued to bicker about Nancy's driving and Monica couldn't have been more relieved when they pulled into Debra Winslow's driveway.

The house was large, as befitted Winslow's wealth and status. Pillars framed the entrance and the front door was flanked by two ceramic Afghan hounds. Considering the circumstances, the silver and gold wreath on the door felt out of place.

They rang the bell and listened as it chimed melodically. Monica was surprised when Debra herself answered the door.

"Oh, Nancy, how kind of you to come." She was wearing a black athleisure suit and diamonds sparkled on her ears and fingers. She looked at Gina. "And Gina." She cocked her head inquiringly at Monica.

"This is my daughter, Monica." Nancy put a hand on Monica's shoulder.

Monica handed Debra the loaf of cranberry bread, which she set down on the foyer table.

She led them into a large living room that was tastefully furnished with neutral-colored sofas and chairs and an Oriental rug of rich blues, reds and greens. A grand piano stood in the corner and Monica thought she recognized a Rothko on the wall.

Monica studied Debra. There was no sign of recent tears, no bags under her eyes suggesting sleepless nights. People grieved in different ways, she reminded herself.

"Such a tragedy," Nancy was saying when Monica turned her attention back to the conversation.

"How long were you and Mr. Winslow married?" Monica watched Debra's expression.

Nancy shot her the look she used to give her when she was a child and forgot her manners.

Debra furrowed her brow. "Let me see." She began to silently count on her fingers. "Let's just say long enough." She barked out a laugh.

"It was a happy marriage?"

That time both Nancy and Gina shot her a look.

"That depends on how you define happy. I was well cared for." Debra's mouth tightened and she clenched her hands in her lap.

"You didn't have children?"

"We really must go. I'm sure you need your rest," Nancy's mother cut in before Debra could answer. She motioned for Monica to get up. "We just wanted to pay our condolences."

"Why were you being so nosy?" she hissed at Monica as they made their way down the slate walkway to the car. "Haven't you learned your lesson? It's nearly gotten you killed before."

Monica feigned innocence. "I was just curious."

"I'm pretty sure Janice would remind you that curiosity killed the cat." Nancy opened the car door. "I know what you're up to. You're not fooling me now any more than you did when you were little and snuck cookies from the cookie jar and told me a burglar had taken them." She paused with her hand on the car door handle. "I know you're going to dig into Winslow's murder and go around asking questions and doing heaven knows what else."

Monica opened her mouth but Gina cut her off.

"You're giving your poor mother nightmares with this sleuthing of yours."

That was rich coming from Gina. She'd been in the thick of it with Monica on more than one occasion.

Nancy put the car in gear and backed down the driveway. "Promise me you'll let the police handle things. That's what they get paid to do, after all."

• • •

Nancy had just dropped Monica off at the farm kitchen to retrieve her car when her cell phone rang. She slipped into the driver's seat, grateful to get out of the cold, and answered the call. She was surprised to hear Tempest Storm's voice come over the line asking if she and Greg were free and could they come for dinner. Tempest owned Twilight, the New Age shop in town. She was something of an oddity in Cranberry Cove, with her unusual style of dress and love of crystals, tarot and all things mystical. The longtime residents were the feet-on-the-ground sort and the most mystical they got was telling their kids that Santa Claus was real.

Monica promised to check with Greg and get back to her. She quickly dialed Book 'Em.

Greg had an estate sale to go to and encouraged Monica to have a girls' night out with Tempest. While she would miss Teddy, the idea of some adult conversation was sorely tempting. Fingers crossed Alice would agree to watch Teddy.

Alice had no problem staying and Monica rushed upstairs to change into something slightly more presentable. She had a momentary pang as she kissed Teddy goodbye but she swallowed it and headed out the door.

It had turned even colder and she put the heater on full blast. Tempest had an apartment above Twilight and Monica found a parking space in front of Gumdrops, but even though it was a short walk, it felt as if the wind was going right through her coat and she was grateful when she reached Tempest's doorway.

Tempest answered the door wearing her customary attire—a long dark blue velvet caftan and a crystal on a silk cord around her neck. Her dark hair, with the broad white streak running through it, was pulled back into a chignon.

"Come in," she said, ushering Monica into the foyer. "I'm so glad you could come. Her voice was deep and mellow. They headed up the stairs to her apartment.

Tantalizing smells drifted from the kitchen and Monica's stomach growled. Tempest led her into the living room, a shadowy cavern with walls painted dark green, heavy purple velvet drapes and furniture that looked as if it would swallow you whole like a Venus flytrap.

Monica perched on the edge of the sofa while Tempest fetched drinks. She returned with a painted enamel tray with two glasses of wine on it. Tempest's hand shook slightly as she handed the glass to Monica.

"I've made a lamb tagine with dried cranberries for dinner." Tempest smoothed a wrinkle in her caftan. "I hope you like it."

Monica smiled reassuringly. "It smells heavenly."

Tempest fiddled with the crystal on the cord around her neck. She seemed nervous. Perhaps she wasn't used to having guests. She didn't seem to have many friends in Cranberry Cove.

"I'd like you to meet someone." Tempest looked into the distance. "He's going to join us for dinner." She swept an invisible hair off her forehead. "But first . . . first I have to tell you the story of how it all came about."

Tempest put her glass on the coffee table and put a hand to her heart. "His name is Emery. And he's my son."

Monica pretended to choke on her wine in order to stifle a gasp. Tempest? A son? Tempest had never mentioned him before, and as far as Monica knew, he'd never visited her in Cranberry Cove either.

"I named him Emery because emeralds are a gem that symbolizes love and romance." She rolled her eyes. "Although he doesn't seem very interested in finding love," Tempest said in the tones of an exasperated mother. "He says he's too busy concentrating on his career."

"But . . . how . . . ?" Monica tried not to stutter but she was dumbfounded.

"I got pregnant at seventeen in my senior year in high school. Or as they used to say in those days, I got knocked up." She shook her head. "It wasn't as common then as it is now with all these stars having a baby first and then getting married." She laughed. "Like the old nursery ditty, *first comes love, then comes marriage, then comes the baby carriage.* Now, it's first comes the baby carriage and then it's a toss-up whether marriage is next or not."

Tempest reached for her glass of wine. "I was meant to be the valedictorian at graduation but instead I was shipped off to my grandmother's in Iowa to await the birth of my baby. There was no question but that it would be put up for adoption."

Monica didn't know what to say. Even after all these years, the pain was evident on Tempest's face. "The father?"

Tempest made a dismissive gesture. "Oh, nothing happened to him. He went on to win the Leadership Award and get a scholarship to college." Her face suddenly brightened and she clasped her hands to her chest.

"My son found me. He said he'd been looking for years but it was one of those DNA tests they sell that finally did it. We've spent the last week together, but today he had some business in Detroit." She glanced at the ornate gold clock on the wall. "He ought to be here any minute now."

Tempest was fetching more wine when the doorbell rang. "There he is." She ran out of the kitchen clutching a bottle of Pinot Noir.

Monica heard voices in the foyer. She tried to imagine what Tempest's son would be like. She pictured him as being tall, with dark hair in a ponytail, wearing a white shirt with balloon sleeves and a purple velvet vest. The picture was so clear in her mind that she was startled when he walked in.

She was right about his being tall and dark-haired but there the resemblance to her image ended. His hair was close-cropped and his dark gray suit, white shirt and blue tie looked as if they were straight out of a Brooks Brothers ad. He was wearing round horn-rimmed glasses and had a silk pocket square tucked into his suit pocket.

"This is Emery," Tempest said, pride making her face glow. "He's the managing director of an accounting firm in Grand Rapids."

He held out his hand and Monica shook it.

"I think the tagine is ready," Tempest said as she motioned toward the dining room.

The table was set with a black and white zebra-print tablecloth, plates with a blue circle in the middle and astrological signs around the edge, and silverware that was slightly in need of polishing. A candelabra with five candles sat in the middle.

Tempest carried in the tagine pot with an air of triumph and set it on the table.

The meal was delicious. Monica couldn't remember the last time she'd had something so complex and exotic, all the flavors blending together in a wonderful harmony. With a new baby, she and Greg were lucky if they had time to roast a piece of chicken and steam some broccoli.

They had just finished their dessert, profiteroles with chocolate sauce, when Emery put his napkin beside his plate and pushed back his chair.

"I'm afraid I have an early meeting tomorrow in Ann Arbor. It's a bit of a drive so unfortunately, I'm going to have to make it an early night." He picked up his plate. "Can I help clear the table before I go?"

Tempest smiled at him indulgently. "You go ahead. We can handle it."

They stood in the foyer as they said goodbye and Monica shivered when Tempest opened the door. She was grateful to escape to the warmth of the kitchen, where she helped Tempest rinse the plates and load the dishwasher.

She was surprised when she looked at the clock. Teddy would

already be in bed and Greg was probably home and searching for something to eat. Suddenly, she was anxious to get back to them.

Tempest walked her to the door. Monica slipped on her coat and was about to say goodbye when Tempest put a hand on her arm. Her expression was troubled.

"He knows," she said in a near whisper, although there was no one nearby to hear her.

Monica frowned. "Who? What?"

"Emery." Tempest's grip on Monica's arm tightened.

"He knows what?"

"Emery knows that George Winslow was his father."

Chapter 8

The house was quiet when Monica got home. Teddy was already asleep in bed and Greg was in the living room watching television with the baby monitor within earshot. He'd already sent Alice home.

He smiled when Monica walked into the room. "How was your evening?"

"Surprising." Monica collapsed onto the sofa next to Greg. "The food was excellent, a lamb tagine."

"Was that the surprising part?"

"No. Tempest had another guest."

"Don't tell me she's found a beau?"

Monica shook her head. "It was her son."

Greg's mouth dropped open. "What? How did we not know?"

"She had him when she was very young—too young to care for him—and he was adopted by another family. He searched for her and only just found her thanks to one of those DNA kits."

Greg whistled. "I've heard of that happening. It's the kind of thing you read about in *People* magazine. Assuming you read *People* magazine."

"I have to admit to peeking at it occasionally when I'm in line at the grocery store checkout."

"I imagine Tempest is thrilled."

"She is. His name is Emery. His adopted parents kept the name she'd given him at birth." Monica laughed. "He couldn't be less like Tempest if he tried. He's an accountant and dresses like he bought all his clothes at Brooks Brothers."

Greg moved closer to Monica and put an arm around her shoulders. "I take it you had a good time?"

"Yes, definitely. But something has me quite worried."

Greg's eyebrows shot up. "What?"

Monica fiddled with a loose thread on her sweater. "George Winslow was his father."

Greg's arm tightened around Monica's shoulders. "George Winslow?"

"Yes. And what's worse is that he knows it."

"You don't think he . . ."

Monica let out her breath in a sigh. "I don't know. But it's certainly possible. And that's what has me worried."

• • •

Monica was feeding Teddy Tuesday morning and idly turning the pages of the *Cranberry Cove Chronicle* when she came upon the headline "George Winslow, A Successful Life." She began to read. It was an ode to Winslow, a "local boy makes good" sort of piece. As the article put it, he was "one of our own." She skimmed through the details of his birth and early childhood in Cranberry Cove, his high school career and his founding of WinGeo Pharmaceuticals.

She was about to fold the paper up when a thought struck her. She quickly turned back to the article on Winslow. According to it, Winslow had married his high school sweetheart, Angela DeBoer. So, Winslow and his ex-wife went to the same high school.

Monica remembered the woman arguing with Winslow at the fundraiser. His ex-wife perhaps? Whoever she was, she certainly had some sort of beef with him. If she could see what Angela looked like . . . Her shoulders slumped. She hadn't gotten a good look at her.

She was changing Teddy's diaper when she had an idea and she thought it just might work.

"Off to work?" Alice said when she arrived and took Teddy from Monica.

"Yes." Monica felt a bit guilty. That wasn't exactly true. She was following up a lead first. Hopefully it would pan out.

Cranberry Cove High School was situated a quarter of a mile outside of downtown. Monica's Focus reluctantly chugged up the small hill leading to the school. She was afraid it was going to be time for a new car soon. Although not brand-new, right off the lot, but something that was used but still serviceable.

The high school had been built in the nineteen-thirties of sturdy red brick and had been added on to over the years as the population of Cranberry Cove grew. Monica pulled into the parking lot and found a space.

The wind sliced through her as she got out of her car. She glanced at the sky. The clouds looked heavy and bloated. More snow must be on the way. It certainly looked as if they'd have a white Christmas.

She felt a stirring of excitement. So many firsts this year. Teddy's first Christmas and their first Christmas in their new house.

She gripped the iron railing as she mounted the cement steps to the front door. She pulled it open and stepped inside. The heat steaming from the old-fashioned radiators nearly made her gasp and she immediately loosened her scarf and unbuttoned her coat.

She'd forgotten how institutional schools used to look—cinder-block walls, worn tile floors. The teachers and administration had done their best to lighten up the place with colorful student artwork pinned to the bulletin boards and a case full of shiny sports trophies.

The office was enclosed in glass and the door was locked. Monica rang the bell and waited. One of the women behind the counter reached for a button, a buzzer sounded and Monica opened the door. She walked up to the counter.

"Can I help you?" a woman with long, curly red hair asked her with a welcoming smile.

Monica cleared her throat. Was she going to come across as some sort of lunatic? What excuse could she give for searching through old yearbooks?

"Do you have copies of past yearbooks?" she finally said, unable to come up with a plausible story. As Gina always said, sometimes bold is better.

Monica could have sworn the woman's eyes narrowed slightly but the smile stayed plastered to her face.

"I'm afraid we don't." She waved a hand as if to encompass the entire building. "We're fresh out of room with the population of Cranberry Cove having grown so much over the years."

Monica's heart sank.

"But the local library does have a collection of all of them going back to the year the school was built. You might want to check there."

"Thank you." Monica gave her a smile that matched hers.

It was a short drive to the library, which was located in an old, converted house. It still had many of the original features, including fireplaces with a delft tile surround depicting various Dutch symbols and scenes like windmills, wooden shoes and fields of tulips. They had all been converted to gas and gave off a cozy warmth on cold winter days.

A balsam garland was spread along the mantel, studded with

shiny, bright balls in gold, silver, red and green. A tree, scenting the room with the smell of fresh pine, stood in pride of place in the center of the room. It was decorated with colorful origami—birds, stars, snowflakes and miniature Santa Claus figures, which had been made by the younger patrons of the library during one of the after-school activities.

Several patrons were slumped over their books in the mismatched but comfortable armchairs scattered around and a young man sat at one of the wobbly wooden tables with thick volumes spread open all around him.

Phyllis Bouma, who had been overseeing the library for several decades, was behind the desk. She smiled as Monica approached. She was wearing a pair of earrings in the shape of bells and her red sweater was appliquéd with reindeer.

"How's Teddy?" she said as soon as Monica reached her. She took off her glasses and let them dangle from the chain around her neck.

She was going to have to get used to that, Monica realized—people immediately asking after Teddy when they saw her.

"He's doing great. He's eating well and finally sleeping for a stretch of five to six hours every night."

"I'm sure that's a relief." Phyllis picked up a piece of paper from the desk, crumpled it up and tossed it in the trash can next to her chair. "Are you looking for a book? Or are you investigating again?" There was a twinkle in her eyes. "I read that George Winslow died and they suspect murder."

"I'm just looking into a few details," Monica said evasively. Anything she told Phyllis would be all over the town by sunset. "I understand the library has an archive of all the yearbooks from Cranberry Cove High School?"

Phyllis cocked an eyebrow at her. "We certainly do. Is there a specific year you're interested in?"

Monica gave her the date and Phyllis slipped out from behind the desk. "Follow me."

She led Monica to a little-visited corner of the library. Books were lined up on the metal shelves, the vivid colors of their spines slowly fading and showing their age.

"I think this is what you want." Phyllis pointed to a row of volumes with the year stamped in gold on the spines. She ran her finger down them and pulled one out. "Phew." She batted at the air. "These certainly need dusting. I think it's been years since anyone has looked at these."

She handed the yearbook to Monica. "If there's anything else you need, just let me know. I'll be back at the front desk."

Monica carried the yearbook to an empty table, pulled out the wooden Windsor chair and sat down. Leafing through the pages brought back so many of her own high school memories. Some things never changed. There were the usual sports pictures, the superlatives — the most athletic, the class clown, the most likely to succeed. It was no surprise that George Winslow had been voted the most likely to succeed. That prediction had certainly come true.

She flipped through the pages until she found the senior portraits and Angela DeBoer's picture. Like so many of the other girls, her hair was flipped on the ends, teased on top and held back with a broad white headband. There was a tiny mole to the right of her mouth, much like the one Cindy Crawford had. She was a pretty girl and Monica could see how she'd managed to attract the boy most likely to succeed.

She rummaged in her purse, took out her cell phone and snapped a picture of Angela's senior portrait, then closed the yearbook and put it back on the shelf.

Hopefully Angela hadn't changed all that much in the intervening years and she'd be able to recognize her despite the time that had passed.

• • •

Monica had saved the business card the photographer at the fundraiser had given her. He'd offered to take pictures of Teddy for a discount if she was ever interested.

His small studio was above a hair salon that was past the harbor and a few minutes outside of town. Monica wrinkled her nose as she climbed the stairs to the second floor. The air was heavy with the acrid smell of permanent wave solution mixed with the flowery scent of hair care products.

Gold letters on the old-fashioned glass office door spelled out *Phil Morris Photographer*. The studio looked dark and Monica felt a pang of disappointment, but she knocked anyway. Moments later she heard footsteps clattering across the wooden floor and the door opened.

Phil Morris looked slightly bewildered, his wispy brown hair awry, revealing a small bald spot on the top of his head. His shirtsleeves were rolled up and the collar was frayed with bits of thread fringing the edge. He blinked rapidly as he stared at Monica.

"I'm Monica Albertson." She stuck out her hand, which he took in a limp grip and gently shook. "You took the photographs at the fundraiser for the Cranberry Cove Animal Shelter."

He was silent for a moment, as if he was running dates and appointments through his head.

"Yes." His eyes widened. "I hope everything was okay. I mean . . ."

"Yes. Everything was fine. I'm trying to track down someone who came to the event. I know it sounds slightly ridiculous but I wondered if you took any other pictures that day besides the pets with Santa Claus?"

"I hope it was okay. I didn't think anyone would mind. Some of the owners asked for pictures of themselves with their pets."

Monica tried to remember if Angela—assuming it was Angela— had had an animal with her. If she had, perhaps she was one of the people who wanted their picture taken together.

"I wondered if I could see some of those photos."

"Yeah, sure." He opened the door wider. "It's a bit of a mess, I'm afraid. When I'm working, I often forget to clean up."

The room was sizeable with a slightly battered-looking wood floor and large windows caked with grime. Pipes ran along the high ceiling. A computer was set on a desk with one leg propped up on a book and a table was scattered with photographs and a cardboard container from a local fast food place. Scrunched-up pieces of paper surrounded the trash can near the desk.

"I added a number of photographs from your event to my portfolio." He slid behind the desk and jiggled his computer mouse. The screen came to life and he pecked at the keys until he found what he wanted.

"Take a seat." He reached behind him and pulled up another wheeled desk chair.

Monica watched as he clicked through the photographs, occasionally raising his eyebrows hopefully. "Anything?"

"Not yet, I'm afraid. This might be a long shot."

"Let's look at the rest of them."

He was about to click to the next photo when Monica said, "Stop," and put out a hand. She inched closer to the screen, studied it and then tapped the monitor with her finger. A woman stood angled toward the camera, one hand on her hip and the other holding a leash. A Yorkie was at her feet, its head turned as if it was looking over its shoulder.

"Can you enlarge it so I can get a better look at that woman's face?"

Phil clicked a few keys and the woman's face came into perspective. She was attractive with high cheekbones, full lips and a small mole to the right of her mouth.

It was Angela DeBoer. It had to be.

What had she and Winslow been arguing about? They'd been divorced for years. Surely, everything had been settled between them.

Or had it?

Chapter 9

Monica couldn't believe it was already time for Teddy's three-month check-up. He had to have put on some weight she thought as she hefted him into his car seat and buckled him in. The time felt as if it was slipping by so fast, she wished she could reach out and grab it to slow it down.

Teddy's pediatrician had retired and his colleague had opened a new practice downtown in an old house that had been refurbished into offices.

The visit went well. Teddy wasn't thrilled when the nurse weighed him or when the doctor put her stethoscope on his chest, but by the time they left, his tears had dried and he had seemingly forgotten all about the traumatic experience.

As Monica had suspected, Teddy had put on weight and grown longer. Pretty soon his three-month onesies would no longer fit.

She snuggled him into his stroller and began to walk toward her car, which was parked in front of Danielle's Boutique. Hammering was coming from a building across the street that had had a *For Sale* sign in the window for months. It looked as if it had finally been rented. Was it going to be another shop?

Her curiosity got the better of her and she crossed the street. She angled the stroller so that she could peer in the window. The floor was covered in sawdust and a workman in overalls was nailing shelving to the back wall.

"It's coming along," a voice behind Monica said. She jumped.

"I'm sorry. I didn't mean to startle you."

Monica recognized him as Jason Vale, the man who had brought the reindeer to the fundraiser.

"No worries. I just didn't hear you coming." Teddy let out a little cry and Monica jiggled the stroller slightly to soothe him. "Do you know what's going in here?"

Vale grinned. "A shop. Mine."

Monica could have sworn he puffed out his chest. "What sort of store will it be?" She could imagine Vale as the owner of a sporting goods store or a shop that sold hunting and fishing gear.

"An apothecary. Medicinal herbs, natural cures." He must have seen the look on Monica's face. He laughed. "I don't make a living taking reindeer to fundraising events. I do a few gigs at Christmastime because the kids love it."

"You don't believe in traditional medicine?"

"I don't believe in pharmaceuticals. Mother Nature has provided us with all the cures we need. Besides, pharmaceuticals are synthetic versions of the real thing. Like the stuff WinGeo pumps out by the bottleful. Why not go directly to the source? His stuff is poisoning people. All you have to do is read the list of side effects."

"When are you opening?" Monica jiggled the stroller again.

Vale made a face. "Whenever the contractor decides to finish up. Hopefully soon. The only thing left to do is to paint the place."

"That shouldn't take long." Teddy began to fuss in earnest. Monica reached down and stroked his cheek. She turned to Vale. "I'd better get going. Good to see you. And good luck with your new venture."

Monica grabbed the handles of Teddy's stroller and maneuvered it across the street and toward their car. Now that they were moving, Teddy was happily kicking his feet and trying to bat at the mobile that hung from the bar of the stroller.

Bart Dykema, who owned and ran Bart's Butcher, waved and rushed out of his shop, the apron around his waist flapping in the breeze.

"My, he's certainly gotten bigger, haven't you, young man." He chucked Teddy under the chin. Teddy's expression was uncertain—to cry or not to cry. In the end, he went back to batting at his mobile.

Bart stuck his thumbs in the waistband of his apron. "I saw you talking to that fella across the street. Something new is going in there. Did he say what?"

"An apothecary."

"An apotha-what?"

"Apothecary. He's going to carry medicinal herbs, he said."

Bart's eyebrows shot up. "I don't see old Doc Fitzpatrick going for any of that nonsense. Especially not when we have WinGeo practically in our own backyard putting out pills to cure everything from gout to halitosis."

Frankly, Monica didn't either, but she didn't suppose Dr. Fitzpatrick's patients were exactly Vale's target audience.

"I'd best skedaddle. There's some lamb that needs cutting up and a couple of orders to get ready. You take care of that baby now."

"I will, don't worry."

Monica continued down the street. She peered into the window of Book 'Em but Greg was busy with a customer. She continued on past the diner, and past Twilight to her car.

She'd have never figured Vale as an herbalist, she thought as she buckled Teddy into his car seat. But as the saying went, looks could be deceiving. He certainly held a negative opinion of pharmaceuticals and WinGeo Pharmaceuticals in particular.

Had he held a negative opinion of George Winslow as well?

• • •

Monica spent the afternoon alternately baking and ferrying the finished products to the farm store. She was exhausted when she got home and barely had time to take her jacket off before Teddy began to fuss for his dinner.

It was a relief to sit on the sofa and feed him. She always found it very relaxing and loved the closeness it provided. Greg arrived home right after she'd finished and was burping Teddy. He looked as tired as she felt. And frazzled. The shop must have been busy.

"A lot of customers today?" She followed Greg into the kitchen.

He leaned against the counter and crossed one leg over the other. "Yes. And Wilma still hasn't shown up. Now I'm officially worried about her. I thought perhaps she was simply being flighty, but that's so unlike Wilma. She's such a levelheaded person."

"I hope she hasn't had an accident." Monica handed Teddy to Greg. "Should we call the hospital? Her next of kin might not have thought to call you. Especially if it's serious. It's hard to think under those circumstances."

A line formed between Greg's eyebrows. "I hope it's nothing like that. But perhaps you're right."

Monica reached for her cell phone. "I'll give them a call."

"Will the hospital reveal that information? They're much more buttoned up about patient privacy now."

"I don't know but they should be able to tell us if she's *not* there. I don't see how that would invade anyone's privacy."

Monica quickly called the Cranberry Cove Hospital. She'd programed the number into her phone when she was expecting Teddy. Her conversation with the person who answered on the other end was brief. Monica shook her head as she ended the call. "They don't have anyone with that name registered at the moment."

"What on earth is going on with her?"

Monica frowned. "I'm going to see if I can find any of her relatives. They might know where she is."

"Good idea."

Monica was boiling some water for pasta and Greg was upstairs putting Teddy to bed when the doorbell rang. She dried her hands on her apron as she made her way to the front door and pulled it open.

"I'm interrupting your dinner," Stevens said as she stepped into the foyer. "I'm sorry."

"We haven't started yet. Please come in. Would you like something to drink?"

"I could use a glass of wine but I shouldn't."

Stevens wiped her feet on the mat and followed Monica into the kitchen, where she collapsed into a chair.

"I have a bottle of Pinot Grigio open, if you'd like." Monica hesitated with her hand on the refrigerator door handle.

"Maybe a little." Stevens massaged her forehead. "It's been one of those days. And tonight is a school concert. Can you imagine what a bunch of five-year-olds are going to sound like? I already have a headache just thinking about it."

Monica put a glass down in front of her and poured one for herself.

Stevens tucked a piece of hair behind her ear. "I came to tell you, we're going to be taking another look at the spot where Winslow's body was found."

"Oh?"

"The ME has finished the postmortem and the findings are curious. First, he was drugged. It appears he was given an antihistamine at a dose that would have made him quite sleepy."

"Was that what—"

Stevens was already shaking her head. "No, it wasn't enough to kill him but more than enough to put him to sleep for a good long while. At first, we thought the aim was to keep him unconscious until

49

he succumbed to hypothermia. And he would have if he wasn't found in time. The temperature went down to ten degrees that night. But that's not what killed him."

"There was all that blood though."

"Exactly. After cleaning him up, the ME found a wound on his forehead that was consistent with being smacked in the head by something. The ME thinks it was a piece of wood, maybe a log or a two-by-four or something like it."

"And that killed him?"

"Yes."

"The ME speculates that Winslow was probably already woozy from the antihistamine he'd been doped with, making it easier for the perpetrator to lure him away from the crowd and deliver a fatal blow with the log."

Monica shivered. "How awful. Who would do something like that?"

"That's what we're going to find out. Stevens downed the last bit of wine in her glass.

Monica raised her eyebrows. "More?"

Stevens pushed the glass away. "No, thanks. All I'd need would be a DUI to make the day complete." She drummed her fingers on the table. "What I'd like to do is take another look at the murder site. Do you think your brother would mind?"

"Jeff? Not at all, but I'll ring him to let him know you're coming."

"Thanks. I don't want him to think I'm an intruder and come after me with a shotgun."

• • •

Monica was glad to collapse on the couch and watch television with Greg, although she was finding it harder and harder to keep her eyes open. Hercule sat up when he saw her and wandered over. He put his head in her lap and she stroked his ears, something he particularly liked. She could have sworn that Mittens gave him a sour look for being so needy as she set about grooming her front paws.

Monica's mind began to wander to Winslow's murder. She was getting more and more worried about Tempest's son. Could Emery have been responsible? She knew he'd been in Cranberry Cove that day and he had a motive, but she couldn't remember ever seeing him at the fundraiser.

But maybe someone else had. She needed a photograph of him to show the people who'd been there. Greg might have seen him. Or Jeff. Or maybe Chelsea. She drummed her fingers on the arm of the sofa. But how to get a picture of him? She could hardly jump out of the bushes or from behind a parked car to snap a candid photo like the paparazzi.

Suddenly it came to her and she jumped up.

"Going to bed?" Greg paused the television program they'd been watching.

"No. I'm getting my laptop. I want to check something."

Monica retrieved her laptop and returned to the living room. She powered it up and typed in the URL for LinkedIn. She put Emery's name in the search bar and waited while the page loaded. She had her fingers crossed that he'd included a photograph with his profile.

The page came into focus and his picture popped up. Monica studied it for a moment. She saw a lot of Tempest in him — his nose and mouth particularly — even if they didn't seem alike in any other way.

She took a screenshot of his photo and sent it to her phone. "Greg?" He turned toward Monica. "This is Tempest's son, Emery. Do you remember seeing him at the fundraiser?"

Greg took Monica's cell and studied the picture. "Was he there? He doesn't look familiar."

"I don't know. That's what I'm trying to find out."

Tomorrow, she'd begin checking with Chelsea and others who had been at Sassamanash Farm that day. Hopefully, someone would remember something.

• • •

Monica arrived at the farm kitchen early Wednesday morning. She wanted to get some work done so she could visit Chelsea later without feeling so guilty about leaving Mick, Janice and Nancy to take up the slack.

It was odd being in the kitchen alone. She rather relished the quiet as she mixed batter for muffins and rolled out dough for scones. By the time the rest of the crew arrived, she was almost ready to cart the baked goods down to the farm store.

She was packing them up when her cell phone rang. She looked at the caller ID. It was Stevens. Was there news? she wondered.

"Morning," Stevens said when Monica answered the call. "My search at Sassamanash Farm yesterday bore fruit. We found the log that was used to kill Winslow. I don't know how my team missed it on the first go-round. It was on top of the woodpile. The ME found traces of blood on it. Winslow's blood. So now we know."

The door opened as Monica ended the call.

"You're early this morning," Nancy said as she took off her coat and hung it up. "Is Greg staying with the baby?"

Monica looked up from the muffin tin she was filling. "Yes. Until Alice arrives."

"Your father never wanted me to work, although a lot of my contemporaries had jobs. Not like in the 1950s and 60s when most women stayed home to raise their family."

"Did you want to work?" Monica dusted the flour off the front of her apron. She'd always had the impression that her mother enjoyed taking charge of the housekeeping, entertaining and having time to lunch with friends.

"Yes. I don't suppose I ever told you but I'd been a copywriter at an advertising agency before you were born. They would have taken me back afterward but your father said no. Sometimes I wish I hadn't listened to him." She reached for the sugar and poured some into a measuring cup. "Of course, I saw how hard it was for my friends who did have jobs when they had children. They worked all day at the office and then went home to cook dinner and bathe the children and put them to bed."

Monica had never known that about her mother. It made her realize how little she actually knew. But did children ever really know their parents? Would Teddy say that about her and Greg one day?

Mick looked up from the dough he was kneading. "Maybe we should advertise. Nancy can write the copy." He gave Nancy one of his blinding smiles.

Nancy's eyes widened. "I could. I know Jeff's wife Lauren has you active on Instagram and all those other places people waste their time on, but why not an ad in the *Cranberry Cove Chronicle*?"

"Why not?" Mick slammed the dough against the counter, then dug the heels of his hands into it.

"I'll have to ask Lauren about it," Monica said. "Meanwhile, I have to run an errand. I hope you don't mind."

"Of course not," Janice said. "You were here early and we're ahead of our usual schedule as it is."

Monica grabbed her coat and slipped into it. She still felt guilty leaving her crew to fend for themselves, but not quite as much as she would have if she hadn't come in early and gotten the day started.

• • •

Several dogs were barking when Monica arrived at the animal shelter. The door to the kennel area was open and she noticed Sharon Dort sweeping the floor. No one was at the front desk so Monica signaled to her.

Sharon gave her a timid smile. She looked as washed-out as she had on Saturday. She leaned on her broom. "You're from the fundraiser, aren't you? Are you here to adopt?"

"Sadly, no. We already have a rescue dog and cat, and with a new baby, I'm afraid there isn't time for another pet." Monica peeked into the kennel. "As much as I'd love to take that little guy home." She pointed to a dog with the face of a Jack Russell but the body of a different breed altogether. It had a bandana with the animal shelter's logo on it around its neck. It appeared to notice Monica's gaze and began wagging its tail furiously, fanning the air in the process.

Sharon smiled. "That's Sparky. His new family is coming to take him home today and he's very excited. Aren't you, boy?"

"That's wonderful." Monica remembered how excited Hercule had been when they brought him home. He was disheveled and in need of a bath, but he was so endearing both she and Greg just melted.

Monica reached in her purse for her phone. "Do you mind if I ask you something?"

Sharon looked doubtful but nodded her head.

Monica pulled Emery's picture up on her cell and held it out to Sharon. "Do you remember seeing this man at the fundraiser? He's probably a few years older now than he was when this picture was taken."

Sharon examined the photograph, then handed the phone back to Monica. "I'm not sure. I might have done. I was quite busy," she said apologetically. "I'm afraid I don't really remember."

"Of course. Is Chelsea in? I'd like to show it to her too."

Sharon glanced over her shoulder, as if she expected Chelsea to magically appear. She ran her hands up and down the broom's smooth wooden handle. "She said she's going to be very busy . . ."

"It will only take a minute. Honest." Monica put a hand to her heart. "Please?"

Sharon lowered her head. "You know where her office is, don't you?"

"Yes." Monica waved a hand in Sharon's direction and began to walk away.

Chelsea jumped when Monica knocked on her office doorjamb. "Can I come in?"

Chelsea had been looking at her phone and quickly shoved it into her pocket. A flush colored her face and she gave a sheepish smile. "I have to confess I was looking at a dating site. I've had no luck meeting men so I thought . . ." She trailed off.

Once again, Monica realized how lucky she'd been to have met Greg.

"I'd love to meet someone like your Greg." Chelsea gestured toward the chair in front of her desk. "But so far no luck." She frowned. "My landlord won't even let me have a pet." She waved a hand, encompassing the animal shelter. "It's why this place is so important to me." She put her head in her hands. When she looked up, tears were trembling on her lashes. "And now Mr. Winslow's wife is contesting his will because she wants the money he left to the shelter. We need that money." She frowned. "The fundraiser was a huge help but it isn't enough to keep us going. I've gone over the budget a million times, but unless that money comes through, we won't last much longer." She covered her face with her hands and it was a few moments before she looked up again.

"I'm sorry. None of this is your problem. Everything just hit me all of a sudden." She sat up straighter. "You wanted to ask me something?"

Monica handed Chelsea her phone. "Does this man look familiar? Did you notice him at the fundraiser?"

Chelsea took a deep breath. "He's cute, isn't he?" She looked at Monica and smiled for the first time. "I don't know. He might have been there, but I'm not sure. So much was going on, what with trying to get that poor Great Dane into its owner's car and the squabble between that bulldog and the boxer." She handed the phone back to Monica. "I'm sorry. I know that's not very helpful. Why do you want to know?"

"Just curious." Monica decided it was best not to reveal her reason for asking.

So, Emery might have been at the fundraiser and he might not have been, she thought as she left the building and went back to her car. She was no further along than when she'd started.

Chapter 10

When Monica arrived at the farm kitchen everyone was clustered around Nancy, who was seated at the table looking as if she was holding court. Her mother always did love being the center of attention.

"What's going on?" She took off her jacket and hung it up. "You all look as if you're conspiring over something. Hopefully, it's not against me." She smiled to show she was joking.

Mick looked over at her. "You know how your mother mentioned advertising? She's come up with a wonderful slogan for our baked goods."

Monica hadn't given any serious thought to advertising. Everyone in Cranberry Cove already knew who they were and what they did. Was it really necessary? Lauren posted on Instagram, Facebook and now Bluesky for them and that drew in the visiting tourists. And as far as she knew, advertising was expensive. The farm was certainly doing better than when she'd first arrived to help Jeff, but there were things that could go wrong. The weather for one. Or a sudden freeze they didn't catch in time. A bad crop. They couldn't afford to splash money around.

She was about to say something when she noticed the smile on her mother's face. She was positively glowing. How could she burst her bubble? She could at least listen to what she'd come up with.

She tried to look eager despite her doubts. "How wonderful. Let's hear it."

Nancy cleared her throat, sat up a bit straighter and threw her shoulders back like an actor about to deliver a monologue. "The slogan is simple but I think it works. Oven-Fresh Every Day." She looked anticipatory, as if waiting for applause.

Monica realized she'd waited a beat too long and tried to make up for it with lots of enthusiasm.

She clapped her hands. "That's perfect. I absolutely love it."

"We can put it on all our products," Janice said with what for her was rare enthusiasm. "On the labels of our compotes and salsas."

"We could even have it printed on our aprons," Nancy said.

What was next? Monica wondered. Were they going to expect her to stand on the street corner downtown wearing a sandwich board?

The more Monica thought about it though, the more she liked it. It wasn't a bad idea really. Oven-Fresh Every Day. It did rather roll off the tongue. She repeated the words to herself as she filled muffin tins with batter and slid them into the oven.

She'd talk to Lauren and see what she thought.

• • •

As soon as the last lot of baked goods was delivered to the farm store, Monica took off her apron and got ready to leave. She wanted to get to Bart's Butcher before he closed. She had a hankering for some pork chops with apples like her Swedish grandmother used to make and she wanted to surprise Greg with a nice dinner.

Lazy flakes of snow melted on her windshield as she drove into town. The lights around the lampposts twinkled in the falling dusk and she felt Christmas in the air.

She parked in front of Gumdrops and began walking toward Bart's, pulling on her gloves as she went. She passed the diner, where, even with the door closed, the smell of sizzling hamburgers and fries drifted out. The scent almost made her change her mind about the pork chops.

A wreath hung from the door of Bart's Butcher Shop and tiny white lights outlined the window. A bell tinkled as she pushed open the door. Bart was behind the counter, a stained apron around his waist and a meat cleaver in his hand. A large roast was laid out on the cutting board.

"Howdy." He leaned both hands on the counter. "What can I do you for?"

"I need a couple of pork chops."

"Bone-in or boneless?" Bart gestured toward the meat case. "Any news about that murder over at Sassamanash Farm? Winslow was a well-known fella in Cranberry Cove. Rich as all get-out but generous. He sponsored the Cranberry Cove High School baseball team. My nephew played shortstop." He frowned. "What was it you wanted again?"

"Boneless pork chops."

"That's right. I've got some beauties for you." He pulled a piece of glassine from a box under the counter and opened the meat case. His hand hovered over several pork chops. "There wasn't much in the *Chronicle*. Do the police have any clues as to who did it?"

Not for the first time, Monica wondered if people really liked talking to her or did they just want to pump her for information.

"You know as much as I do, I'm afraid."

"It must have been awful frightening, uncovering a dead body like that." He chuckled. "But then you've uncovered your share of corpses, haven't you?"

Monica gave a thin smile.

Bart plucked two chops from the case. "I've got some beauts for you here." He tilted them toward Monica. "Will these do you?"

"Perfect."

He tore a piece of butcher paper off the roll on the counter and with practiced ease, wrapped up the chops and tied them with string. He plunked the package into a brown paper bag and handed it to Monica.

She passed him her credit card and waited while he ran it through the manual imprinter. He refused to upgrade to something newer even though most of the other stores in Cranberry Cove had gotten on the bandwagon and switched to credit card readers. Danielle's had even begun accepting some of the phone payment apps.

Monica thanked him, took her package and went back out the door, which tinkled again as it closed behind her. She glanced down the street and noticed her stepmother, Gina, was standing on the sidewalk in front of her shop, Making Scents, in just a sweater and a pair of pants. She had her arms wrapped around herself for warmth and appeared to be assessing her current window display. She turned, noticed Monica and waved.

Monica joined her in front of the window, where Gina had arranged a glittering display of essential oils in jewel-toned bottles. They were set out on a red velvet cloth trimmed in fake fur.

"What do you think?" Gina's teeth were beginning to chatter.

"It's lovely. You've done a splendid job."

"I'm pleased." She took Monica's arm. "Come in and get warm for a bit. Estelle is here."

Estelle was Gina's mother-in-law. She'd arrived in Cranberry Cove in September and had decided to stay through Christmas before going back to Florida. Despite her fears, she and Gina had hit it off immediately and it was easy to see why.

Even though Monica had only been outside for a short while, the heat inside Gina's shop felt heavenly. "It smells like a Christmas tree in here." The shop was small and she didn't have to look around to see there were no trees in sight, unless Gina had secreted one in the stockroom.

"It's balsam fir essential oil. We were going for a Christmas vibe, right, Estelle?"

"Absolutely." She turned to Monica. "Good to see you." She held out a hand with long acrylic nails painted bright red.

She was dressed for the season in red leggings and a sweater with bells around the neck and cuffs. Gina was looking equally festive in red leather pants and a sweater with a Christmas tree made of silver sequins.

"I heard you found another dead body at your brother's farm." Estelle gasped dramatically and her hand flew to her mouth. "How terrible for you."

"It was a shock," Monica admitted. And that was the understatement of the century, she thought.

"I knew his ex-wife." Estelle fiddled with one of the bells on her sweater.

Monica was confused. "Whose ex-wife? George Winslow's?"

"Yes. I grew up in Cranberry Cove. Didn't you know that? Angela and I both went to Cranberry Cove High. We were on the cheerleading squad together."

Monica tried to picture Estelle in a cheerleading uniform, shaking pompoms and yelling *go team go* but failed.

"Winslow was the quarterback and that's how the two of them met. They were together from then on." She held up two fingers intertwined with each other. "Angela was very pretty and all the boys in school were after her, but she fell for George right off the bat." She rolled her eyes. "He was very handsome, dark hair, brooding eyes and a great physique." She sketched an upside-down triangle with her hands. "They married right after high school. Neither set of parents was too happy about it, that's for sure."

"Did you and Angela stay in touch?"

Estelle nodded. "Yes. We weren't best friends but we got together for lunch occasionally, although after I moved to Florida, not so much. An email here and there, an annual Christmas card, that sort of thing."

"Were you surprised when she and Winslow divorced?"

"I sort of saw the writing on the wall. I tried to tell her but she wouldn't listen. She insisted everything was fine." Estelle shrugged.

Monica raised an eyebrow.

"Angela worked as a gal Friday in the office of a manufacturing plant in Grand Rapids, helping to put George through college. She took a course to become a medical assistant at night and when he graduated, she got a job in a doctor's office."

"What was Winslow doing?"

"He'd become a sales rep for a pharmaceutical company. Finally, he was making some good money. Angela was talking about starting a family but then the bomb hit."

"A bomb?"

"Yes. In the form of Debra Kowalski, former weather girl from a station in some two-bit town in Montana. She'd finally scored a job with WZZZ in Grand Rapids as a reporter and that's when she and Winslow met."

"Had Winslow started WinGeo yet?"

Estelle tucked a hair that had escaped from her updo behind her ear. "Yes, shortly before that. Angela was looking forward to quitting her job and then pffft, Winslow up and left her for a weather girl. Can you imagine?"

"Angela must have been furious." Gina fiddled with one of the bottles on the counter and the scent of lavender drifted on the air.

"She should have been but she was more in the dumps than anything. She let herself go, stopped touching up her hair and nails. She even lost weight. She looked like a clothes hanger. It was a shame. She'd always had a nice curvy figure." Estelle patted her own hips.

So not angry, Monica thought. Could a depressed person be aroused to murder? Especially after all these years?

Chapter 11

It was almost closing time as Monica headed back to her car. Lights were blinking out in several shops already. Snowflakes swirled in the wind coming off Lake Michigan and Monica picked up her pace. She was about to open her car door when Hennie motioned to her from the window of Gumdrops.

"Hello, dear," Hennie said as she ushered Monica inside. "A bit nippy out there, isn't it?"

"Yes." Monica smoothed down her hair. It was always a challenge to tame her curls and the wind hadn't helped.

The shop smelled sweet and sugary with candy arranged in a colorful array along the wall. It reminded Monica of the penny candy in the shop around the corner when she was growing up. Finding a penny on the sidewalk meant you could buy a piece of candy, and finding a nickel was a real bonanza.

The colored beads hanging in front of the door to the stockroom rattled and Hennie's identical twin, Gerda, appeared. As usual, they were dressed alike in tartan plaid skirts, boiled wool jackets and pristine white blouses with Peter Pan collars.

"Such a shame about the incident out at the farm. How are you holding up, dear?" Gerda smoothed the pleats in her skirt. "I heard from Mrs. Koster that you're the one who found the body." Her eyes gleamed with curiosity.

Hennie snorted. "What does Mrs. Koster know? Her daughter says she's getting dementia."

"This time she's right. I did uncover the body." Monica thought about the dollar bill she'd been chasing. What if she'd let it fly away? Winslow's body might not have been discovered until the snow melted. Had the killer been counting on that?

Gerda put a hand on Monica's arm. "I'm so sorry that happened to you."

"And what a nasty thing to happen to George Winslow," Hennie added. "Not that I knew him. Not really. But his company created a lot of jobs in Cranberry Cove and people are grateful for that."

"Did you know his former wife?" It was a long shot Monica thought, but the Van Velsens seemed to know everyone in town, both young and old.

"No," Hennie and Gerda said at the same time.

"But we did know the second wife, although not well." Gerda fiddled with some boxes of Droste pastilles arranged in a display on the counter.

"We were in the choir together at St. Andrews, although she was an alto and we were sopranos."

"You don't think she . . ." Hennie clamped her lips shut.

Gerda glanced at her. "There was something going on though. Don't you remember . . ."

Hennie frowned. "You mean . . ." She swept her hand toward the wall. "Mr. Bateman?"

"Yes."

"Who is Mr. Bateman?" Monica looked back and forth between the two sisters. She was lost.

"Mr. Bateman rents an office above Danielle's. He's a divorce lawyer," Gerda said with a certain amount of relish.

"And we've seen Debra Winslow visiting his office on more than one occasion," Hennie added.

Monica's mind was racing. "You think Debra planned to divorce her husband?"

"I don't know what else she'd have been doing up there." Hennie shifted from one leg to the other. "Darned sciatica." She put a hand to her back.

"Maybe she was having an affair?" Monica pictured a suave lawyer in a custom suit, and a swanky office with a plush sofa and mood lighting at the touch of a button.

Both Hennie and Gerda burst out laughing.

"With Mr. Bateman?" Gerda wiped her eyes. "Good heavens, no."

"He's almost as old as we are, is balding and has terrible false teeth," Hennie said.

"So you think she was planning to divorce her husband?"

"It seems likely, doesn't it?"

• • •

Monica was starting dinner and Teddy was in his carry cot cooing and kicking his feet when Greg got home. Snowflakes clung to the shoulders of his coat and were quickly melting in his hair.

"The snow's picking up," he said as he hung up his coat. "And the temperature has dropped again." He kissed Monica on the cheek and she let out a squeal at the touch of his cold skin.

"Has Wilma shown up yet?" Monica reached into the bin in the pantry and pulled out an onion.

Greg grimaced. "No, and now I'm really worried. I tried calling the number she gave as an emergency contact but the line's been disconnected. I can't think of what's gotten into her. She's always been so reliable, I'm afraid this means something has happened to her."

"Should we alert the police?"

"It's not really our place, but there doesn't seem to be anyone else who realizes she's gone missing."

Monica couldn't imagine being so alone in the world that hardly anyone would notice she'd disappeared.

"I'll call Detective Stevens in the morning and see what she thinks." Monica began slipping the peel off the onion. "I talked to the Van Velsens today."

Greg's eyes twinkled. "Oh? What's the latest gossip? Anything juicy?" He picked up one of the apples Monica had set out and rummaged in a drawer for the peeler. He brandished the piece of fruit. "I might as well make myself useful."

"According to the Van Velsens, Winslow's current wife has made several visits to a divorce lawyer with offices above Danielle's."

"Does that rule her out as a suspect? If she was already planning to divorce Winslow, what would be the point of killing him?"

"I don't know." Monica paused with her knife in her hand. "I looked it up and Michigan isn't a community property state. If she divorced him, a judge would be the one to decide how much she gets in the settlement. And considering Winslow's influence, a judge might lean in his favor." Monica put the knife down. "And maybe she signed a prenup and wants more. With Winslow dead, she probably assumed she'd inherit his entire estate. Don't prenups expire if you're still married to your spouse at the time of death?"

"I gather he was worth a lot. He must have been with his shares in WinGeo."

"Yes, even if he does leave half of it to the animal shelter." Monica scooped up the chopped onion and put it in the pan heating on the stove. "Chelsea said Debra Winslow is contesting the will. Chelsea would be devastated if Debra won."

"What would that mean for the shelter?"

"I don't know. They're scrambling now to raise money and Chelsea wants to expand." Monica added the pork chops to the sizzling skillet.

"It doesn't make Chelsea look good." Greg began to work on the apple, a long ribbon of peel dangling from the fruit.

"No, it doesn't. But other people also had a reason to want him dead. Like Emery." Monica put the lid on the pan. "For Tempest's sake, I hope he had nothing to do with it."

"Those pork chops are beginning to smell good." Greg lifted the lid and peered into the pan. "What about the ex-wife?"

"I don't know. They've been divorced a long time. But who knows? He ditched her just when he was starting to make money and life was getting good."

"Maybe something triggered her after all these years." He looked at Monica's face and raised his eyebrows. "You're going to try to find out, aren't you?"

"Am I that transparent?"

"Frankly, yes." Greg laughed but then his expression turned serious. "Just be careful, okay?" He put his hands on Monica's shoulders. "Stick to doing research online and at the library. Things that aren't dangerous."

"Don't worry. I'll be careful."

Greg shook his head. He didn't look convinced.

• • •

Thursday morning, Monica was taking inventory of needed supplies and making a list and Janice and Mick were working on the first batch of cranberry muffins when the door opened and Nancy breezed in, her face flushed from the cold.

"Good morning," she called out as she took off her coat and hung it up. "What shall I do?"

"Good morning." Monica put down her pad and pen. She gestured toward the corner of the kitchen. "There's a batch of salsa ready to be labeled."

Nancy rubbed her hands together. "The cold is making my arthritis act up."

"If you'd rather not—"

Nancy waved a dismissive hand at Monica. "It's fine. Don't worry."

"Use 'em or lose 'em is what they say. Isn't that right?" Janice shook her finger at Nancy. "You should try magnets. They helped my cousin Etta. She swears by them. You put them wherever the pain is."

Nancy laughed. "At my age, you have pain all over. I'd need an awful lot of magnets. I might end up sticking to the refrigerator." She carried the carton filled with jars of salsa to the table. "Too bad the labels don't have our new slogan on them. Oven-Fresh Every Day."

"We have to use up the ones we have and then I'll order some new ones." Monica ripped the sheet of paper off the pad and put it by her laptop. "I'm sure Lauren would design us something eye-catching."

The kitchen fell quiet as they each worked at their respective tasks, moving around each other as if they were performing a choreographed dance.

Monica pulled the first batch of muffins from the oven and put the pan on a rack to cool. She looked over at her mother and noticed she looked quite pale. She supposed it was the contrast between now and how she'd looked when she'd come in rosy from the cold.

"Oh, dear," Nancy said suddenly.

Monica stiffened. "What's wrong?"

"It's my heart." Nancy put a hand to her chest. "It's beating too fast." She gasped and Monica felt a surge of alarm.

"Is there anything we can do?" Mick put down the rolling pin he was holding. He looked at Monica. "Should we call an ambulance?" He pulled his cell phone from his pocket.

Nancy shook her head. "No, no, I'll be fine. I forgot to pick up my pills from the pharmacy and I didn't have any left for this morning."

Monica was already taking off her apron. "I'll go get them for you."

"I'm sure I'll be fine," Nancy said with her hand pressed against her chest.

Monica gave her the same look her mother used to give her when she suspected she was lying.

"Nonsense. I'll do it." She pointed at the jars Nancy was labeling.

"Those can wait. Put your head down and rest." She grabbed her coat and dashed out the door before her mother could protest any further.

She tried to be mindful of the speed limit as she drove into town but several times she found herself several miles over and had to slow down. She hadn't realized her mother had any trouble with her heart. She had to pay more attention. It had been so scattered lately with the new house and the new baby.

The pastel-colored shops along Beach Hollow Road went by in a blur as she scanned the block for a parking space. She smacked the steering wheel in satisfaction when she noticed a pickup truck backing out of a space right in front of the drugstore. She waited impatiently while he put the vehicle in gear and finally pulled away.

She shot into the space a bit too quickly and hit the curb, but she barely noticed it as she jumped out and ran into the drugstore. She made her way down the aisle, past the shelves of Christmas lights and ornaments, past the small collection of rubber flip-flops, half-deflated inner tubes and pool noodles on clearance and toward the back of the store. Her mother might be downplaying her heart issue but she wasn't taking any chances.

No one was waiting at the counter and she stepped up briskly. The pharmacy assistant looked at her a bit strangely and she realized she was panting. It seemed an eternity before the young woman came back with a small white paper bag that rattled slightly as she put it down on the counter.

Monica paid for it, dashed out of the store and into her car, thanking her lucky stars that she'd found such a great parking space. She put her key in the ignition, turned it and waited. Nothing happened. No sound of the engine coming to life, just the click of the key turning in the slot.

Despite the cold, perspiration broke out and trickled down her back. It would take forever for the garage to send someone to tow it. Maybe there was someone around who could help. Greg had dropped his car off at the garage that morning for maintenance and Monica had driven him to work, so he wouldn't be able to help.

She was about to phone Mick and ask him to rescue her when there was a tap on her window.

"Do you need help?" Jason Vale was peering at her.

"Yes." Monica would have jumped for joy if she hadn't been in the front seat of her car with the seat belt on. "My battery is dead." Monica frowned. "I hope it's not too much trouble. Is your car parked nearby? It's just that I'm picking up my mother's pills and she needs them right away." Monica tapped her chest. "For her heart."

"No need for another car. I have the perfect thing. It's a portable battery jumper. It's new and I've been dying to try it. I'll be right back." He winked.

Monica phoned the farm kitchen while she waited. Her mother was feeling a bit better. Resting was helping. Monica wondered if working at the farm was too much for her mother. Her mother insisted it wasn't and that she didn't know what she'd do staying home all day. She wouldn't let Monica pay her so Monica bought her gift certificates to the Clip and Curl Beauty Salon, Bart's Butcher and occasionally one for Danielle's Boutique. Although her mother made a fuss about accepting them, Monica knew she appreciated the gesture.

She was ending the call when Vale arrived back holding a machine with various clamps attached to it. She got out of the car and watched while he raised the hood and attached the clamps to various parts of the engine. If this worked, she might get Greg one of these gadgets for Christmas. She nearly cheered when her engine turned over and the car roared to life.

She leaned out the open car door. "I can't thank you enough." She reached for her cell phone, which she'd tossed on the passenger seat. She hadn't asked Vale yet whether or not he'd seen Emery at the fundraiser.

She pulled up the picture she'd put on her phone and held it out to Vale. "Do you remember seeing this fellow at the pet and Santa event?"

Vale took the phone from her and studied it. "I'm not sure." He scratched his head. "But I think I did see him. I thought it was odd."

"Why?"

"Because he didn't have a pet with him. That was the whole point, wasn't it? Why else show up?"

Monica felt her heart sink. Tempest had just been reunited with the son she'd given up as a baby. Was he about to be taken away from her again?

• • •

67

By lunchtime, Monica was exhausted. The scare with Nancy had taken more out of her than she'd realized. Fortunately, the pills she'd picked up from the drugstore had helped and her mother was back to her old self—slightly bossy and occasionally judgmental.

She was hungry too. The scent of sugar, vanilla and cinnamon hanging in the air was making her mouth water. She thought about grabbing a cranberry muffin or scone but knew that wouldn't be enough. What she needed was a bowl of the diner's chili—the chili that wasn't on the menu and that only locals knew about.

"I'm running to the diner to grab some chili. Can I bring anyone anything?"

Mick jerked a thumb toward the refrigerator. "I brought my lunch. I have some avgolemono leftover from dinner I'm going to heat up."

Janice's head jerked up. "What on earth is that. It sounds like a disease."

Mick laughed. "It's soup. It's like your chicken soup but with rice, lemon and egg yolks."

Janice shuddered. "Give me a can of Campbell's chicken noodle soup any day. I don't want any of that foreign stuff. It's sure to give me heartburn." Fortunately, Mick had a thick skin and simply laughed.

"I brought a sandwich," Nancy said.

"Me, too." Janice dusted off her hands and opened the refrigerator door.

"I'm off then. I won't be long."

Monica buttoned up her coat, pulled on her gloves and waved as she went out the door. She held her breath as she turned the key in the ignition of her Focus. Fortunately, the engine hummed to life and she was on her way.

It was noon when she pulled into a parking space along Beach Hollow Road. The delicious aromas from the diner drifted down the street and she hastened her steps. She could almost taste the chili and she couldn't wait.

The buzz of conversation and clanking of dishes and silverware floated out the door as soon as she opened it. Several people were sitting at the counter hunched over their plates and most of the booths were full. The poor harried waitress was racing to one of them, plates of hamburgers and sandwiches balanced on her arms.

Gus gave her a small smile from his place behind the grill, barely breaking rhythm as he flipped burgers and plunged baskets of fries into a vat of boiling oil. Monica was proud that she had progressed from no recognition from Gus when she'd arrived in Cranberry Cove, to a discreet nod and now a smile. Once, when she'd been pregnant with Teddy, he'd even said a few words to her, but that had obviously been an extenuating circumstance.

Monica was debating whether to order take-out or wait until one of the stools became vacant when a hand shot up and beckoned her, its owner not clearly visible over the back of the booth, but judging by the size of the cocktail ring on its finger and the length of the nails, it had to be Gina.

Monica had to dodge the waitress as she made her way to the booth and slid into the seat opposite her stepmother. Gina was idly stirring a spoon around and around in a bowl of tomato soup.

The waitress breezed by, plunked a glass of ice water in front of Monica and asked if she was ready to order. Monica had barely finished speaking before she took off at a trot to serve another customer.

Monica looked at Gina. She didn't seem like herself. Her usual spark was missing.

"Are you okay?"

Gina let out a long sigh.

"What's wrong."

"Estelle. That's what's wrong."

"I thought you two got along."

"We did. We do. But now she's saying she's not going back to Florida but is moving to Cranberry Cove full-time."

"Isn't that good news? You'll be able to spend more time together."

Gina wrinkled her nose. "She wants to stay with me and Micky. Until she finds a place of her own." Gina let the soup spoon drop into the bowl. "She wants to redo everything I've done. The couch isn't soft enough, the arms on the chairs are too low, the light in the kitchen isn't bright enough." Gina slammed her hand down on the table. "She even wanted us to move out of the master bedroom and into the guest room so she'd have more space."

"That is asking a bit too much." Monica leaned back as the

waitress slid a bowl of chili with two packets of crackers perched on the saucer onto the table. "Don't you think she'll get bored here in Cranberry Cove? All her friends are in Florida. I know she's mentioned a mahjong group she plays with as well as a pickleball team."

"That's what I told her." Gina picked up her soup spoon. "But she said she's going to be busy here running her new business."

Monica's eyebrows shot up. "New business?" Steam was rising from Monica's bowl of chili. She scooped up a spoonful and blew on it.

"Yeah. She wants to buy Bijou, the jewelry store across the street, only she wants to sell costume jewelry."

"I know she joked about buying that spa you used to drag me to, but costume jewelry? Few women in Cranberry Cove have any use for real jewelry, let alone paste. People go there for engagement and wedding rings, maybe a cross for a Christening gift and occasionally a fiftieth wedding anniversary present."

"She thinks it will attract the tourists. She may be right. Look at Danielle's Boutique. All those expensive clothes. Who buys them? It's the tourists who keep her in business. Estelle thinks they'll do the same for her."

"Has she already bought the shop?"

Gina shook her head. "No, not yet. All I can hope for is that the deal falls through."

● ● ●

Monica was ready to call it a day. She looked at her watch and groaned. It wasn't time yet. They had to finish up the last batch of baking to stock the shelves at the farm store. There was always a crowd that stopped by after work to pick up something fresh to take home. Her mother's slogan suddenly came to mind. Oven-Fresh Every Day. It was certainly true. Not all companies could make that claim. Certainly not the company that made that lipstick she bought. It claimed to *Last Through Every Kiss.* It hadn't lasted for an hour.

She was filling the cart with the finished goods for Janice to deliver when her cell phone rang. She thought she recognized the number. "Hello?" she said somewhat uncertainly.

"Monica, it's Stevens." Her voice sounded as weary as Monica felt. "I have a question for you. Do you remember if Winslow ate or drank anything at the fundraiser?"

Monica grimaced. She tried to picture the scene that day but all she could conjure up was a slide show of brief snapshots.

"I'm afraid I don't remember."

Stevens's sigh came down the line. "I knew it was a long shot." She paused. "Do you remember that bottle we found alongside Winslow's body?"

Monica pictured it in her mind. "Yes."

"The results came back from the lab. It didn't contain the antihistamine that knocked Winslow out, as we had thought it might. It had been washed and any trace of the substance it had once contained was long gone. And this is the interesting part, the bottle was one used by WinGeo for cough syrup. But a long time ago. The product had been taken off the market and the design of subsequent bottles of cough syrup was different. More modern, according to the current marketing director. What the significance of leaving it by his body was, we still have no idea."

Monica thought about it as she hung up the call. She had no idea either. It seemed bizarre. Was the killer trying to send them a message?

Chapter 12

The table was set, lentil soup was waiting in the slow cooker and Teddy was happily babbling in his carry cot. Monica perched her laptop on the kitchen table and opened it. She smiled as it powered up and her screen saver, a photograph of Teddy, materialized.

George Winslow was killed for a reason, she thought. She just had to figure out the reason. She decided to look the company up and see if anything came to light.

The results of her search began to slowly appear. She scrolled through the articles until one in particular caught her eye. It was from the *Cranberry Cove Chronicle* and the headline read, "Geosinex Taken Off Shelves." She began to read.

> *WinGeo Pharmaceuticals has agreed to take their drug Geosinex, used to treat coughs, off the market after numerous side effects were reported. A woman, who prefers to remain anonymous, claims they weren't warned of one of the side effects — that Geosinex might cause drowsiness. She holds Geosinex and WinGeo Pharmaceuticals responsible for her husband's death. Shortly after taking a dose of the cough syrup, he fell asleep at the wheel, veered off the road and crashed into a tree. He was pronounced dead at the scene. "He never would have driven, had he known," she said.*

Monica was so engrossed she didn't hear the door open and was startled when Greg appeared in the kitchen.

"Whatever that is you're reading must be very interesting." He bent down to pet Hercule, who was nudging his leg with his snout while Mittens looked on from a distance.

Monica gestured toward her laptop. "I'm reading all these complaints about WinGeo and their products. Their over-the-counter cough syrup had to be taken off the market when it was discovered it contained codeine. After 2017, cough syrup with codeine was prescription-only."

"Are you thinking that's somehow relevant to Winslow's murder?" Greg bent and smiled at Teddy.

"I don't know. In another article, a woman blamed WinGeo's cough syrup for her husband's death. Drowsiness wasn't listed as a side effect and he fell asleep at the wheel and crashed into a tree. What if WinGeo hadn't actually changed the formula of that cough syrup but had simply put it in a new bottle and claimed it had no codeine even though it did? That would be criminal and could be a motive."

"Is there any way to find out if that woman attended the fundraiser?"

Monica shook her head. "I'm afraid not. The article doesn't give her name. Besides, there were a number of other people making complaints as well."

Greg pointed to the slow cooker. "Soup?"

"Yes. Lentil."

"It smells delicious. I'm going to go wash my hands."

Monica sat for a bit longer. She rubbed her forehead as she scrolled on her laptop. She pictured all the people who had been at the fundraiser. Any one of them might have been disgruntled with WinGeo for one reason or another. Or even Winslow personally. Were they looking for a needle in a haystack?

• • •

Alice breezed in early Friday morning, stamping her feet on the mat and shaking out her hat.

"The storm they talked about on the weather last night has started. It looks to be a bad one. The weatherman said it was lake effect snow so it's going to pile up quickly and might affect visibility. They showed the radar screen and my, the storm certainly looked angry. Not that I could make heads or tails of all the swirls of purple and green."

She bent down and unzipped her boots, placing them side by side by the door. "I'll never forget that blizzard that hit us in January 1978. I was working as a nurse at the hospital at the time. The storm was so bad the second shift couldn't get there so we all had to stay. They even locked the doors so we couldn't leave. When I finally got out, it took me three hours to clear my car off, and when I finally got home, I couldn't open my front door until I'd shoveled away some of the snow."

"Let's hope this storm isn't going to be anything like that." Monica paused to listen to the baby monitor but the rustling sound she'd heard had stopped. "We probably won't get many customers at the store today. I may be bringing home a lot of cranberry muffins and scones."

Alice smiled. "Nothing wrong with that."

Monica slipped on her coat. "I'd best be off. It's easier to leave if Teddy isn't awake. Does it ever get any easier?"

"I'm afraid not." Alice gave a knowing smile. "At least not when they're little."

Monica said goodbye and headed out to her car, which was already covered in snow. She retrieved a scraper from the backseat and began to clean it off. By the time she was finished, her hands were freezing despite her gloves and she was quite sure her face was bright red from the cold.

She started to head toward the farm but then changed her mind. They really wouldn't need to do as much baking today so they'd be fine without her for an hour or two. She wanted to chat with Angela Winslow, née DeBoer, to see if she could get some information from her. There was just one problem. She had no idea where Angela lived.

There had to be a way to find out. Too bad the telephone white pages were extinct. Or were they? She nearly stopped short when the thought occurred to her and she mentally apologized to the fellow behind her when he had to slam on his brakes as well.

There had to be an archive of white pages somewhere. Maybe with someone who never threw anything out? Or . . . maybe the library had some. They had Cranberry Cove's yearbooks so perhaps the idea wasn't so far-fetched.

She pulled into the nearest driveway she came to, turned around and headed back toward town.

• • •

The library looked especially cozy with the snow falling outside the window, gas fires in the fireplaces and the lights on the Christmas tree twinkling. Phyllis Bouma was busy arranging books on a cart, her bright red reading glasses perched on the end of her nose. She looked surprised when she saw Monica.

"What are you doing out in this filthy weather? Fortunately, my house is only a block away so I don't have to worry about getting stuck in the snow."

"I don't envy you the walk home." Monica had gotten chilled just going from the parking lot to the front door of the library.

"With a warm jacket, hat and mittens, I'll hardly feel the chill." She placed her hands down on the books in the cart. "Now how can I help you?"

"I was wondering if you had an archive of telephone white pages. I thought since you had those yearbooks—"

Phyllis pursed her lips. "We do but I'm afraid it's not complete. Do you need a specific year?"

"I'm on something of a wild-goose chase, I'm afraid. I'm counting on this person having stayed at the same location for some time."

"Who is it? I might know her." She laughed. "Although I'm not as good as the Van Velsen sisters." She led Monica to the back of the library and a shelf lined with directories. "They know *everybody*."

"I'm looking for Angela Winslow. She was Angela DeBoer before she married."

Phyllis scrunched up her face. "I'm sorry, no. I don't know her." She pulled a volume of white pages off the shelf. "Is this about George Winslow's murder?" Her eyes gleamed.

Monica was loathe to admit it but she had no choice. She couldn't come up with a suitable fib. "Yes."

"Helping the police with their inquiries, are you?" Phyllis laughed. "I think I've been watching too many British detective shows. They're frightfully good," she said in a fake British accent. "I hope this helps." She handed Monica the volume in her hand. "There are . . . let me see . . . one, two, three more." She patted Monica on the shoulder. "Good luck. I'd better get back to the desk. Not that I anticipate getting many visitors in this weather. I told Flo to stay home. No point in risking the trip when we're unlikely to be busy."

Monica carried the first volume of white pages over to an empty desk. Dust rose up as she opened it and she had to stifle a sneeze.

She turned first to the page of names that began with *D* and ran her finger down the column. There were numerous people with the last name DeBoer but none were named Angela. She flipped to the back of the book and the *W*s. A third of the way down the page an

Angela Winslow was listed. There were no others. It had to be Winslow's ex-wife.

Monica pulled out her phone and put the address in her notes. She'd better hurry before the storm got any worse and the roads became impossible.

• • •

Monica had to clean off her car again when she left the library. An inch of snow had already accumulated on the roof, windshield and hood. She wondered if she ought to go home. The plows and salt trucks wouldn't be out for a while yet and she didn't want to get stuck.

She started the car and had to immediately turn on the windshield wipers as the snow pelted her window. She knew the neighborhood Angela lived in and it wasn't far. She decided to chance it.

She turned onto the street with a grateful sigh. She'd made it. She crawled down Butler Lane searching for the house number. Some were prominently displayed while others were coy, hiding behind overgrown bushes or trees. The metal numbers at one house were nailed to a board and two of them had come unmoored and were dangling upside down.

Finally, Monica found the address she was looking for, a small Cape Cod–style home painted light green. A curtain in one of the windows twitched. Good. Angela was at home.

The path to the front door was already covered in snow. Monica paused for a moment admiring the scene — pristine snow covering the yard and clinging to the bushes. She made her way to the door and rang the bell.

The door squeaked as it was opened and a woman stood peering at Monica through the screen door. She had hair dyed dark brown, pale skin and the telltale beauty mark at the side of her mouth.

"Yes?"

"I was wondering if I could talk to you for a moment about your ex-husband, George Winslow."

Angela pushed the screen door open. "Come in." She had a small dog in her arms. He stared at Monica with wary eyes.

Monica stepped inside. She was grateful to get out of the cold. She bent to remove her boots but Angela stopped her.

"Don't bother with that. This old carpet has seen worse than a bit of snow. Princess here has done her business on it more than once. Haven't you, you precious girl." She kissed the top of the dog's head. "I suppose you're from the papers. Winslow's murder was front-page news."

Angela had obviously mistaken her for a reporter. This might be easier than she'd feared.

"I hope you don't mind if I ask you a few questions."

"Not at all. I've spoken with a couple of reporters already and they all insist on painting Winslow as a saint. Which he wasn't." She turned to face Monica, her expression intense. "He was a cheapskate through and through. I want the world to know who and what he really was, so go ahead and write about it or blast it on television. I don't care."

Monica was really intrigued now. George Winslow a cheapskate? That didn't square with the man who donated so generously to the Cranberry Cove Animal Shelter.

Angela led her into a small living room, the type that used to be called a parlor. There was a large picture window draped with lace curtains, a sofa covered by a crocheted afghan and an armchair with a sagging bottom. Monica perched on the sofa and Angela sank into the chair.

"What do you want to know?" Angela said as soon as she sat down.

Monica wished she'd prepared better. She didn't even have a pad and a pen. Did reporters still use those or did they tape interviews with their cell phones?

Angela didn't seem to notice anything amiss so Monica plunged in. "Did you and Winslow stay friends after your divorce?"

Angela sneered. "Friends? Heck, no. We didn't have any children so there was no reason to. Besides, he was a jerk."

"A jerk?"

"Yeah. We struggled in the early days. I worked as a gal Friday while he went to school. There was no question of my going to college. George was the smart one. I just got by."

Princess jumped into Angela's lap and she stroked the dog's head. "We lived in a crappy apartment near the campus and I commuted every day from Lansing to Grand Rapids. It's a miracle I made it back and forth in that piece-of-junk car, which was all we could afford."

Monica made sympathetic noises but she didn't have to say anything. Angela didn't need any prompting.

"Then finally, he graduates. Hallelujah! We could get out of that miserable apartment and I was able to go to school to become a medical assistant. Don't get me wrong. We weren't exactly rolling in it, but compared to the way we'd been living it was like we'd suddenly won the Power Ball.

"George gets a job as a pharmaceutical rep. He's making decent money and we can afford to go out to eat once in a while—nothing fancy, just places like IHop and once for our anniversary we went to Red Lobster."

Angela started to get up. "Listen, would you like something to drink? I could make some tea."

"I'm fine. Thank you." A cup of tea really did sound good but Monica didn't want anything to interrupt Angela's flow.

Angela flopped back into her chair, which groaned alarmingly. "Then George started his own company. WinGeo Pharmaceuticals. He had to get his name in there somehow." She chuckled. "It wasn't long before he was making more money than ever. That's when that woman blew into town. Like something out of the *Wizard of Oz*."

Monica had a sudden mental image of the Wicked Witch. "That's when he met his current wife? I guess it would be more appropriate to say widow."

"Yes. Debra. She should be glad he's dead. She's getting a bit long in the tooth and in my opinion, it was only a matter of time before he began shopping for a newer model." Angela shifted in her chair. "For her sake, I hope she didn't sign a prenup."

"Oh?"

"George was more tight-fisted than Scrooge. Look at how I ended up." She waved a hand around the room. "You should see where he and Debra lived. It's not fair. I worked to put him through school." She stabbed her chest with her index finger. "I was the one who made the sacrifices. She just waltzed in and took advantage of everything I'd worked for."

The movement startled Princess, who jumped off Angela's lap and stood glaring at her.

"Sorry, baby." Angela made cooing sounds at the dog.

Monica had half expected Angela to be resigned, to let bygones be bygones, but it was clear she still harbored a burning resentment against her ex-husband.

"Scrooge. That's what George Winslow was. Put that in your report so people know what he was really like."

"That is certainly a different picture of the man. But he is leaving half his estate to the animal shelter so he obviously has a soft spot."

Angela snorted. "Can anyone prove that? For all we know, he just said that to make himself sound good."

"You were at the shelter fundraiser, weren't you?" Monica chose her words carefully. "I think I saw you there."

Angela rolled her eyes. "You must have seen me arguing with George then. I don't know why I bothered. He's said no every other time I've asked him. Why would this time be any different?"

"You had something to ask him?"

"Yeah. For the last few years, I've been pleading with him to raise my alimony. Look at this place." She waved her hand around the room again. "The carpet needs replacing, the sofa is stained. He hadn't been making nearly as much money when we divorced."

"Doesn't a judge have to make the decisions about alimony?" Monica knew nothing about matrimonial law but that seemed likely.

"Yeah. I was asking him to give me more money out of the goodness of his heart. He'd hardly miss it. What was I thinking? The man had a heart of stone."

Chapter 13

The snow had begun to blow, obscuring the road as Monica headed back to the farm. She glanced at her speedometer. She was going barely fifteen miles an hour. At this rate, it would be dark before she got home. Someone in a sports car whizzed past her and she wasn't surprised when a mile further on she saw him stuck in a ditch.

She was coming to the hill leading away from the center of town. She imagined her car sliding out of control down it and her heart began to pound. Snow continued to blow, making it hard to follow the road, and the windows were fogging up. She turned on the defroster and mercifully a small circle of clear glass appeared, and eventually the entire window was free of fog.

She started down the hill, clutching the steering wheel tightly. The wheels lost traction, the car spun and began heading down the hill sideways. Monica tried not to panic. Steer into the skid, she kept reminding herself. Although that had always seemed counterintuitive to her. Fortunately, there were no other cars on the road, everyone having had the sense to stay home.

She reached the bottom of the hill, the wheels gripped again and she was able to right herself. She was trembling by the time she reached the farm store.

She was hardly surprised to find the parking lot empty except for Nora's Taurus parked in her usual spot.

She opened the door and stood on the mat stamping her feet to get the snow off. Nora was sitting at one of the café tables reading a book.

She looked up. "Oh, it's you. I thought we had an intrepid customer who was so enamored of our cranberry muffins that they had to brave this foul weather to satisfy their craving."

"Has anyone been in at all?"

"Nary a one since the storm started."

"I propose we close up and go home. If we can get there." Monica pulled off her gloves. "Let's split up what's left in the case. I know your boys like the cranberry-orange cookies so why don't you take those. And some scones for your breakfast tomorrow." Monica reached across the counter for a piece of glassine. "I'll grab a few things for Alice as well, and Greg loves the cranberry bread."

They each filled bags with their choice of baked goods. "The boys are going to be thrilled," Nora said as she bagged the last cookie.

"I hope those won't spoil their appetite."

"Are you kidding? Their stomachs are caverns. There's no filling them up. They've barely gotten up from the dinner table when they start looking in the refrigerator for something to eat. My food budget is probably higher than the GDP of some small countries."

"Let's go home now," Monica said as she cinched her bag closed. "I hope you can make it."

Nora reached for her boots and began to tug them on. "I should be okay." She put on her coat, pulled on her gloves and wrapped a scarf around her neck. "Having lived in Michigan my whole life, a little snow doesn't scare me. You be careful."

"I will." Monica pulled her cell phone from her purse and dialed the farm kitchen. Mick answered and she told him to send everyone home.

She was about to head back out to her car when the door opened. Surely not a customer. "Jeff!"

Snow clung to his knit cap, covered the shoulders of his parka and was melting on his eyelashes.

"What are you doing here?" they said at the same time.

"I came to send Nora home and to close up," Monica said.

"And I came for the same reason. I was on my way back to our cottage when I noticed the light was still on. I couldn't believe Nora was still here."

Monica took note of the dark circles under Jeff's eyes and the tense set to his mouth. He started to say something but then clammed up without a word.

"What is it?" Monica frowned. She hated seeing her baby brother in misery. Not that he was a baby anymore—he was a grown man—but she felt the same responsibility for him now as she had when he was a toddler.

"I'm thinking of selling the farm," he blurted out, not looking at Monica.

Monica felt the blood drain from her face. She felt dizzy and her stomach began doing somersaults. "But what . . . why? The farm is doing well and is on a solid footing." Monica had been doing the bookkeeping for Jeff since she'd arrived in Cranberry Cove. The farm had been on shaky ground then, thanks to the caregiver embezzling from Jeff while Jeff was in Afghanistan, but it was now decidedly in the black.

"I owe it to Lauren. I want to give her a better life."

"She knew what the life would be like when she married you. Has she told you she's dissatisfied?"

"Not exactly." Jeff toed the floor with his boot. "But I've seen her looking at social media and what her friends are doing—nice houses, fancy trips, expensive jewelry. I can't give her any of that."

"Has she said she wants that?"

"Not in so many words. But if I sold the farm, we could move to Chicago like she'd planned before we met. She'd easily find a job at a real marketing firm and I'd . . . do something."

"That was then. People's desires change. How do you know she even still wants that?" Monica paused but Jeff didn't say anything. "I can answer that. You don't."

"You think?" Jeff's face brightened slightly. "You think she's okay living like this?"

"Yes. I've never heard a word of complaint from her. You have to stop torturing yourself and talk to her."

Jeff sighed. "You're probably right. I've gotten myself all worked up over nothing."

"So, you'll talk to Lauren? I'm sure it will put your mind at ease."

Jeff grinned. "Okay, sis. I get the message. I'll talk to her tonight."

• • •

The storm had started to abate by the time Monica headed home. It was still snowing but she was able to turn the windshield wipers down a notch. She barely noticed the passing scenery as she drove away from the farm. Had Jeff been serious about selling? She couldn't imagine life without Sassamanash Farm. It had become as much a part of her as her arms or legs. Would she and Greg be able to secure enough money to buy it themselves?

Her only hope was that Lauren would reassure Jeff and convince him she was perfectly content and this whole notion of selling would blow over.

The plows had obviously been out earlier but there was already a thin layer of snow covering the macadam. Monica prayed black ice wasn't hiding underneath. The car fishtailed a bit as she pulled out onto the main road but she was able to get it under control.

She held her breath as her car inched up the hill and breathed a sigh of relief when she reached the top. A little further and she'd be home.

She pulled into the garage alongside Greg's car, which was still partially covered in snow.

Greg was in the kitchen with Teddy asleep on his shoulder. "I sent Alice home early. I hope she doesn't get stuck."

Monica pulled off her hat and shook it. "It's letting up and the plows and sanders have been out so I think she'll be okay."

"I closed the store since the only person who came by was the postal carrier. And he wasn't interested in buying any books, although we did have a nice chat and we wished each other a merry Christmas. I think he was glad to get in out of the cold for a few minutes."

"Still no Wilma?" Monica bent down to take off her boots.

"No." Greg's expression turned serious. "I think it's time we called the police. If we're out of line, at least we can say we tried to do something."

"I agree. If Wilma was the flighty type, that would be different."

Greg nodded. "You can practically set your watch by her."

"I'll give Stevens a call as soon as I get these boots off."

Monica set her boots on the mat, hung up her coat and pulled out her cell phone. She plopped down on one of the kitchen chairs. She hadn't realized how tense she'd been until now. She took a few deep breaths and clicked on Stevens's number.

It rang several times before Stevens answered. There were noises in the background and the sound of people speaking. Stevens said she was at a crime scene but nothing major—someone had vandalized a mailbox. She wasn't far and said she'd stop by and take Monica's report.

At least Stevens didn't tell her it was none of her business, she thought as she hung up.

Monica was making some tea when the doorbell rang. Hercule was roused from sleep and raced to the door to vet the caller. Monica grabbed his collar as she swung the door open.

Greg must have heard the bell too because he came downstairs holding Teddy.

"He's starting to look like you, Greg," Stevens said as she loosened her scarf.

"Come into the kitchen. I have some tea brewing."

"That sounds heavenly." Stevens followed Monica into the kitchen. Greg joined them and Monica poured out cups of tea.

"What's this about your assistant disappearing?" Stevens picked up her cup and turned to Greg. "What's her name?"

"Wilma Butkus. She's been working for me for a couple of years now. It's completely unlike her. She never missed a day of work and was totally reliable."

Stevens frowned. "When was the last time you saw her?"

"At the fundraiser for the shelter at Sassamanash Farm. I thought perhaps she'd gotten tired and had gone home but the next day she didn't show up for work."

"Did something happen that might have upset her?"

Greg's ears turned slightly pink. "No," he said, but Monica could tell he was thinking about Wilma trying to kiss him. "Not that I know of."

Stevens had pulled a pad of paper and a pen from her pocket. "What's her address?"

Greg glanced at Monica. "I don't know. I'd have to look it up. I have it at the store."

"But she lived in Cranberry Cove?"

"Yes."

"Do you know of any family? Friends?"

Greg looked sheepish. "I'm afraid not. I never asked her. I suppose I should have." He put his face in his hands. "Wilma was just *there.* Like the display table or the checkout desk or that armchair with the saggy seat." He looked up. "I feel terrible. I should have shown more of an interest in her. I guess I took her for granted."

"Do you have any reason for thinking she may have come to harm? She's an adult. She has a right to take off if she wants, even if it is rude not to let you know."

"Wilma wouldn't do that," Greg said firmly. "She was devoted to her, er, job."

"You've tried the hospital?"

"Yes. No luck."

"Do you have a photograph of Wilma?"

Greg shook his head but Monica held up a hand. "Wasn't she in one of the pictures you took at that book signing you held? She wanted a photograph of herself with that thriller writer who had to have a particular brand of bottled water and you had to order a whole case?"

Greg made a face. "How could I forget. I'll go get my phone. I left it upstairs."

He returned with his cell, brought up the picture and handed it to Stevens. She glanced at it.

"Thanks. Text it to me and I'll get it circulated." She drained the last of her tea. "And don't forget to get me her address. I'll send someone to check out her house, make sure there are no signs of a break-in or any indication she's been abducted." Stevens began to get up.

"Is there anything new on the Winslow case?" Monica had taken Teddy from Greg and was standing up, gently rocking from side to side.

Stevens made a face. "That case gets more puzzling by the minute. I suspect you know as much as I do." She gave a teasing smile.

Monica decided she'd best come clean. "I did talk to his ex-wife, Angela," she admitted. "She had an argument with Winslow at the fundraiser over her alimony. She wanted more money and he refused."

"Thanks. That's helpful. I'll arrange to interview her tomorrow."

Monica felt a pang of guilt as she said goodbye to Stevens. She hadn't mentioned Emery and his connection to Winslow. She tried to convince herself that it wasn't relevant but failed. Why had Emery been at the fundraiser? And without a pet? It was certainly curious.

• • •

Monica couldn't believe it had already been a week since she had found Winslow's body. The image flashed through her mind and she shuddered as she carried Teddy downstairs to feed him. His hair was ruffled with sleep and she couldn't resist running her hand over it.

Greg had pancakes cooking on the griddle and the aroma of frying bacon was in the air. Yesterday's storm had blown over and the skies were blue and cloudless. Sun glinted off the glossy carpet of snow and slanted through the kitchen window. Monica felt her spirits lift immediately.

"Are you working today?" Greg said as he filled two plates with pancakes and bacon and carried them to the table.

"Yes." Monica put Teddy on her shoulder and gently patted his back. "We're anticipating a good crowd today. We've been busy all week long with gawkers coming to the farm store hoping to catch a glimpse of where the murder took place, although yesterday's storm put even that crowd off. Fortunately, they're also gobbling up cranberry goodies at a brisk pace."

As soon as Alice arrived, Monica headed out to the farm kitchen. She'd just opened the door and flicked on the lights when her cell phone rang. She glanced at the number. It was Chelsea.

"Monica, this is Chelsea. I have a huge favor to ask you."

"Oh?"

"I think I left my scarf in the barn at the farm the day of the fundraiser. I wouldn't bother about it but my grandmother knitted it for me and I've had it for years."

"I'll look for it as soon as I have the chance."

Chelsea thanked her and Monica ended the call. She debated going to search for the scarf immediately but decided to get some baking done first. She was trying something new—cranberry-walnut sourdough bread. By the time she'd set the dough aside to rest, Mick, Janice and Nancy had arrived.

It wasn't long before the kitchen was filled with the scent of cranberry scones, muffins and cookies baking. Monica began loading the cart to wheel everything down to the farm store in time for the morning crowd.

Nora was starting the coffee when Monica opened the door. Nora rushed over to help. She held the door while Monica bumped the cart over the threshold.

"Did you get home okay yesterday?" Monica said as they began arranging the baked goods in the case on the silver platters Monica had snapped up at an estate sale.

"Yes, and then I got stuck at the end of our driveway of all things. Our neighbor Stan came out to give me a push, bless his soul. He's not getting any younger and you know what they say about performing physical activity in cold weather and how it can lead to a heart attack. He's a big bear of a guy so I suppose it wasn't actually that hard for him." Nora picked up the last two scones and topped the pyramid she'd been making. "How about you? Did you get home okay?"

"Yes. Those all-weather tires we bought were definitely worth it." She set out the remainder of the muffins and stood back to admire the effect.

Monica left the cart at the store to pick up later and made her way across the field toward the barn. There were deer tracks in the snow and more than one set of footprints crisscrossed the field. Monica stepped in one and wasn't surprised to see it was substantially larger than her own. Jeff and his men probably went back and forth this way several times a day.

The door to the barn squeaked when she pulled it open. All the farm equipment had been put back inside and it was hard to imagine this was the same place that had been transformed into the North Pole. Monica couldn't imagine how they would have missed seeing Chelsea's scarf when they moved all the props out of the barn, but she searched anyway.

She diligently peered into every corner. She knew what it was like to lose a sentimental object. Her grandmother had made her a rag doll and she'd carried it everywhere with her, slept with it and even held it in her lap when she ate. She'd insisted on taking it with her in spite of her mother's objections the time they went to the Museum of Science and Industry in Chicago. She'd stopped to play with one of the interactive exhibits and in her haste to see what was next, had left her doll behind. She'd been heartbroken.

So far her search hadn't turned up the missing scarf and she was beginning to despair. She hoped it hadn't been carried away with the props. A flash of white caught her eye, but it was just an oily rag that Jeff must have used to wipe his hands when repairing the equipment.

She was relieved when she finally spotted something hanging off the seat of one of the cranberry beaters and was relieved to see it was Chelsea's scarf.

It was beautifully knitted in an intricate pattern of cables with knotted fringe on the ends. No wonder Chelsea was upset thinking she'd lost it. Monica picked it up and fingered the soft wool. Cashmere? She tucked it into her pocket and headed out of the barn.

She retrieved the cart from the store and began to walk back to the kitchen, snow crunching under her feet. She heard an engine roaring as she approached one of the bogs. The bog had been flooded at the beginning of the season and was now covered in a thick layer of ice. A truck was slowly making its way across the bog, laying down sand as it went. Jeff was behind the wheel and waved when he saw Monica. There was always something to do on a cranberry farm. The sand would sift down onto the vines as the ice melted, nourishing them and keeping out weeds.

She continued down the path and finally reached the kitchen. The walk had warmed her up and she quickly unbuttoned her coat as soon as she was inside. She took Chelsea's scarf from her pocket and laid it on the table.

Nancy leaned over it. "Isn't that lovely. That's a beautiful stitch."

Janice walked over with a bowl in her hands. "You know what they say about knitting."

Monica tried not to roll her eyes. "No, what do they say?" She knew Janice was going to tell them no matter what so it was useless to protest.

"If you gift a significant other a sweater you knitted yourself, they will break up with you."

Monica closed her eyes and took a deep breath. Finally, she said, "Fortunately, it's not a sweater and Chelsea's grandmother knitted it for her, not a significant other."

Janice shrugged. "I'm just telling you." She turned on her heel and went back to the counter.

"She must have been desperate when she realized she'd lost it." Nancy fingered the scarf gently.

"Or, she lost it because she was desperate."

Nancy raised her eyebrows but Monica didn't elaborate. She was wondering if Chelsea had indeed been desperate, was it because she had killed Winslow and was desperate to get away?"

• • •

Monica was glazing a batch of cranberry scones when Chelsea called asking if Monica had found her scarf. Monica felt a wave of guilt. She should have called Chelsea immediately to tell her the good news. She promised to drop it off as soon as she finished with this last batch of baking. It was close to lunchtime and she could pick up something to eat at the diner.

It felt blessedly cool outside. In spite of the large fans that had been installed, the kitchen could feel as hot as a ninety-degree summer day.

The roads were considerably clearer than the day before, with the plows, the sand trucks and the morning sun having melted a lot of the snow. Monica glanced out at the lake as she passed it. The large balls of ice that had formed along the shore looked like giant bowling balls and thick slabs of ice reached out into the water like fingers.

Monica pulled into the parking lot of the animal shelter. She noticed the paint was peeling where the sun hit the wood and the sign above the door was missing a letter. No wonder Chelsea had been desperate to raise money. She picked up Chelsea's scarf, which she'd wrapped in some tissue paper, and locked the car. She heard dogs barking as soon as she approached the door.

The reception area was clean with slightly worn furniture and with the smell of disinfectant lingering in the air. No one was at the front desk so Monica peered through the window in the door behind the desk hoping to catch someone's attention. She recognized Sharon Dort, who was swabbing the floor with an old-fashioned string mop, swishing it back and forth across the tile. A bucket of gray water was in the corner.

Monica knocked on the glass and Sharon looked up. She leaned the mop against the wall and pushed open the door.

"I suspect you're here to see Chelsea."

She was wearing a faded flowered top and blue pants that were baggy in the knees. Her pale brown hair was threaded with gray and held in place behind her ears with bobby pins.

"I'm returning Chelsea's scarf." Monica put the tissue-wrapped bundle on the desk. "She left it at the farm the day of the fundraiser."

"Thank you so much. Chelsea was that upset when she realized it was missing. It means a lot to her." She traced a scratch in the wooden desk with her finger. "I made a scarf for my hubby. We were just dating then, or stepping out as my grandmother used to call it."

Monica thought of Janice's pronouncement about knitting a

sweater for a significant other. Perhaps the curse didn't extend to scarves.

"He treasured that scarf and wore it from then on." She chuckled. "He was always sad when he had to put it away for the summer. I wanted to knit him something for warmer weather to replace it, but you don't really wear knitted garments then, do you?"

Monica shook her head.

"When he died, my Albert, I buried him with that scarf. I knew he'd want it with him."

"I'm sorry."

Sharon sighed. "It was a car accident that took him. He fell asleep at the wheel of the car and hit a tree. He died instantly. It never should have happened." She shook her head.

The door opened and Chelsea came in, bringing a gust of cold air with her.

"I brought your scarf."

"You found it!" Chelsea's eyes lit up. "Thank you so much for bringing it, but you didn't have to. I would have come to get it myself."

"No problem. I wanted to pick up some lunch in town anyway. It feels good to get out of the kitchen. I needed a break."

Monica couldn't help but think about Sharon as she pulled out of the shelter parking lot and headed back toward town. There was an air of sadness about her, an air of heaviness that enshrouded her. She wondered how long ago her husband had passed away.

The story of his accident sounded familiar. Had she read something like that in a book? She was currently rereading Jane Austen's *Sense and Sensibility* so it couldn't have been in that. She was pulling into a parking space in front of the hardware store when it occurred to her. There had been that story in the *Chronicle* about WinGeo's cough medicine and how one woman blamed it for her husband's death when he fell asleep at the wheel.

Was it possible that woman was Sharon Dort? She was going to have to look into it further. Because if it was Sharon, then she too had a reason to want Winslow dead.

Chapter 14

The noon whistle sounded just as Monica reached downtown Cranberry Cove. Her stomach growled as if on cue and she laughed. It was time to get something to eat. A Reuben sandwich from the diner sounded good. As a matter of fact, her mouth began to water at the very thought.

Beach Hollow Road was crowded with people out doing their shopping. There was a line at the counter in Bart's Butcher Shop and there was even a small crowd in the Golden Scoop ice cream parlor despite the frigid outdoor temperatures.

She found a space at the end of the row of shops in front of Making Scents, Gina's aromatherapy store. She wondered if Jeff had talked to Gina about selling Sassamanash Farm. It was worth asking her. The thought that he might go through with it haunted her. She hoped he'd talk to Lauren soon.

She opened the door to Making Scents and inhaled the mingling perfumes of lavender, eucalyptus, patchouli and other heady aromas. Almost immediately she felt her shoulders relax and her breathing slow.

Gina was waiting on some customers, a middle-aged couple in expensive coats standing very close to each other.

Monica wandered around the shop, sniffing the various bottles. She was partial to lavender but had come to appreciate the properties of some of the other oils. Peppermint essential oil had helped with morning sickness when she was pregnant with Teddy, and she'd been very grateful to Gina for the suggestion.

The door swung open, startling Monica. Estelle waltzed in carrying a bag from the Purple Grape, the wine shop down the street. She was wearing a white fake fur jacket that made her look somewhat like a polar bear.

She smiled and gave Monica a hug. She held up her shopping bag. "I'm celebrating." She pulled a bottle halfway out of the bag. "Champagne."

"What are you celebrating?"

"It's a done deal. I've bought Bijou. The owners finally agreed to my terms."

Monica wasn't surprised. She could imagine that Estelle's negotiating style was somewhat like being hit by a battering ram.

Estelle swept a hand toward a display of oil diffusers. "That looks so much better over there, don't you think?"

Monica glanced at Gina, who must have heard because she rolled her eyes. Obviously, the rearrangement had been Estelle's idea, not hers. Monica was sure Gina was going to be glad when Estelle was busy with her new shop.

"I'm going to put this in the fridge to chill." Estelle disappeared through the door to the stockroom.

Monica went back to studying Gina's two customers. Gina had mixed some lavender oil with a carrier oil and had dabbed it on the woman's neck. The man pressed his nose close to her neck, closed his eyes and inhaled.

The woman giggled. "Let's dribble a bit of this into our bath tonight."

"I can't wait," he said in a husky voice.

The woman turned her head and it struck Monica that she recognized her. It was Debra Winslow. She didn't know the man. He had sandy blond hair that hung over his collar in the back and there was an unusual smell clinging to his coat. Something antiseptic. Monica had smelled the odor before but she couldn't place it.

Gina pulled a glossy Making Scents shopping bag out from under the counter, wrapped several glass vials in tissue paper and carefully placed them inside.

"And these." The man handed Gina two lilac-colored hammered glass bottles with diamond-cut ball stoppers.

Debra leaned her head on his shoulder as she waited for Gina to ring up the sale. It was obvious they were more than casual acquaintances who happened to bump into each other. Winslow had only been gone a week and it looked as if his wife had already moved on.

• • •

In the end, Monica never did talk to Gina. Instead, she followed the man who had been so cozy with Debra Winslow in Gina's shop. She didn't know what she hoped to gain but her intuition told her it would lead to something.

He and Debra had split up on the sidewalk after a brief kiss and had gone their separate ways. Monica didn't know what she'd do if he jumped into a car and drove off, but it would clearly be game over. But he didn't. He continued down the street to an older house that had been converted into offices. Monica knew it well. Teddy's pediatrician was located in the same building.

She slipped through the door just before it closed behind him. He punched the elevator button, loosened his scarf and pulled off his gloves as he waited, whistling tunelessly and tapping his foot. The elevator door opened and Monica slipped in in back of him.

She was quite sure he hadn't seen her in Making Scents but she kept her head down, pretending to look at her phone, as they made their way to the third floor. The same smell she'd noticed clinging to him was fainter now but still there.

As soon as the elevator doors opened, it hit her — she knew what the smell was. It was the odor that every dentist's office she'd ever been in had had, and it was coming from the office down the hall. The man strode briskly to the door and pulled it open. Monica waited until it closed and then read the gold lettering on the glass. Owen Evans, DDS.

Was the man who'd been with Debra the dentist or a patient? Monica hesitated then reached for the door handle. The receptionist was on the telephone but looked up and smiled when Monica walked in. Monica looked around the small waiting room, where chairs with chrome armrests were lined up along one wall that was hung with photographs of people flashing huge white smiles.

An older woman was seated in one of the chairs but she didn't see the guy who'd been with Debra. She caught a flash of white and a man in a medical coat passed the open door to the reception area. It was him. Had Debra been a patient of his?

The receptionist ended her phone call and looked at Monica with her thinly penciled eyebrows arched.

"Can I help you?"

"I'd like to make an appointment to have my teeth cleaned."

It had been an impulsive decision but Monica hoped the hygienist would be the chatty sort. They often were. And she really was due for a cleaning so what was the harm?

• • •

Monica always found kneading dough to almost be like meditation. Her hands were busy and thoughts floated through her mind like a leaf riding on a breeze. One by one, the suspects in Winslow's murder crossed her consciousness until she hit on Emery.

She had to admit, she hoped he wasn't the murderer, but the fact that he was seen at the fundraiser without a pet was definitely peculiar. She hoped he had an alibi. Was there some way she could find out? She didn't want to ask Emery himself. What would he think? And she didn't want Tempest to be any more alarmed than she already was.

Perhaps a bit of research was in order. Emery had said he came to Cranberry Cove partly for work. He'd even mentioned a business meeting in Ann Arbor. Could she call his secretary and ask about his schedule? It would be unlikely that she'd be in the office on a Saturday but it was worth a try.

As soon as the cart had been loaded with baked goods and Janice had left to wheel it down to the farm store, Monica pulled out her cell phone. She typed LinkedIn into the browser and put Emery's name in the search bar.

His résumé was impressive. Monica scanned the entries. It seemed he was currently working at Morgan Financial as a senior vice president. Monica found their website and made a note of the telephone number. She wasn't particularly hopeful, but she made the call and waited. And waited. Finally, an answering machine picked up, directing her to leave a message and assuring her that someone would get back to her at the earliest possible opportunity. She ended the call. So much for that. She'd do some searching on her laptop when she got home.

● ● ●

Hercule was beside himself with excitement when Monica opened the door. His tail wagged furiously and he looked at her with those big dark eyes that had won her over the moment she saw him. She knelt down, hugged him and then scratched behind his ears. Mittens strolled over to say hello as well, rubbing up against Monica's legs and purring loudly.

Alice watched Monica, smiling indulgently. "Teddy's napping. He's been an absolute angel."

"I can't thank you enough." Monica slid out of her jacket. "I never worry knowing that Teddy is in good hands."

"My pleasure." Alice retrieved her coat from the closet, put it on and began to pull on her boots. "I'm off to do some Christmas shopping. Wish me luck. My grandson wants some electronic device I've never heard of and don't even know what it does, but hopefully I can find a kind salesperson willing to educate me."

Monica said goodbye and quickly closed the door. It was still freezing out and spring was a long way off. She cocked an ear toward the baby monitor. Silence. She carried it into the kitchen with her and got out her laptop.

A Wikipedia entry popped up first. Monica scanned it, but there was nothing there that would serve as an alibi. Emery was quoted in a few other articles about finance, but that wasn't useful either.

Monica scrolled through the remaining entries and was about to go to the next page when Emery's picture popped up alongside an article about a recent conference in Detroit where Emery was the keynote speaker. She ran her finger down the article until she came to the date. It was the same day as the fundraiser. Could Emery have made it back from Detroit in time to murder Winslow?

She entered the name of the conference — Your Finances in 2025 — into the search bar. She hoped there would be a website and that it hadn't been taken down yet. She almost squealed when the website popped up.

Emery was prominently featured and he'd delivered not just the keynote speech but several lectures during the course of the day. There was no way he could have made the trip to Sassamanash Farm in time to have any involvement in Winslow's death.

Monica didn't realize she'd been holding her breath until she let it out in a whoosh. She could cross at least one suspect off her list.

• • •

With Christmas quickly approaching, the stores in downtown Cranberry Cove were staying open later on Saturday nights. She still had Christmas shopping to do herself. Although Teddy was too young to understand the meaning of Christmas, she thought he might enjoy seeing all the sparkling lights. And as a bonus, she could fetch some dinner for Greg. With Wilma's absence and someone temporarily hired in her place, he didn't feel confident about leaving the store.

She fixed herself a quick meal of a grilled cheese sandwich and tomato soup she'd made with some of the tomatoes from their garden that she'd canned.

She downed her dinner, cleaned up and got Teddy ready to go. Hercule looked forlorn as she closed the door but she assured him that she would take him for a ride as soon as she could. Teddy seemed excited, kicking his feet and waving his arms as she strapped him into his car seat.

Lights twinkled in the distance as she approached Beach Hollow Road. She suspected that all of the parking places would be taken but there was a tiny lot behind the Pepper Pot and Mickey said she was welcome to park there anytime.

Teddy was dozing when she went to take him out of his car seat. His eyes flickered open and then closed again as she transferred him to his stroller. So much for showing him the Christmas lights.

People scurried back and forth on the sidewalks, their arms burdened with shopping bags, murmuring *Merry Christmas* to those they passed. Monica looked around appreciatively. The air was festive with all the lights circling the lampposts and the excited chatter of the shoppers.

She walked down the street, pausing to look in shop windows. She'd reached the end of the commercial area of Beach Hollow Road before making any decisions about what to buy for whom. She pulled her list from her pocket, where she'd sketched some ideas. She thought Gina might like a scarf from Danielle's and perhaps a sweater for her mother and a crystal from Twilight for Janice. Then she still had Mick and Nora to think about, not to mention Greg. Why were men always so difficult to buy for?

She wheeled Teddy's stroller back down the street until she came to Twilight. Tempest was restocking the glass cabinet where she displayed a sampling of different crystals.

Her face looked strained, and although it was hard to be sure given the caftan she was wearing, Monica thought she looked as if she'd lost weight. She smiled at Monica and Teddy but it appeared to be an effort.

Monica leaned on the counter. "You're still worried about Emery, aren't you? You haven't talked to him about his alibi or Winslow's murder?"

Tempest let out a sigh. "No. I'm almost afraid to ask if he has an alibi. What is he going to think? His mother is worried he might have committed murder?" She gave Monica a sharp look. "Do you know something?"

"Yes, and it's good news. Emery has an alibi for the entire day of the murder."

All the muscles in Tempest's body seemed to let go at once. Her face relaxed and she grabbed the counter for support. "He does? How do you know?"

"He was at a daylong conference in Detroit. He was the keynote speaker and also gave several lectures. There's no way he could have made it to Sassamanash Farm."

Tempest grabbed both of Monica's hands. "Thank you." She closed her eyes briefly. "You don't know how much better that makes me feel." She smiled and put her hands on the counter. "I don't suppose you came here just to tell me that. Is there something I can do for you?"

With Tempest's help, Monica chose a lovely piece of amethyst, a crystal believed to protect against negative thoughts. Monica had to suppress a smile. Janice certainly needed it. Perhaps it would keep her from making all her dire and mythical predications.

"This is perfect." Monica accepted the bag from Tempest, wished her a merry Christmas and left Twilight. She and Teddy made their way down the street toward Book 'Em. She'd ask Greg if he wanted something to eat.

She was nearing the diner when the door opened and a man emerged carrying a paper bag with a grease stain slowly blossoming on the front. "Hey." He shifted the bag from one hand to the other. "How are you? I'm sorry, I've forgotten your name."

"It's Monica. How is your new shop coming along?"

"Great." Vale grinned. "Just great. Down to the finishing touches now."

"When do you open?"

"When everything is done." He let out a laugh. "And who knows when that will be. But I'm in no hurry, fortunately." He shifted from one foot to the other. "I hope you'll stop by. I'm planning a grand opening." He laughed again. "Although how grand it will be, I don't know. Probably some appetizers and an assortment of drinks. No musical talent, I'm afraid."

"I'll definitely try to make it."

"I'm glad I ran into you. There's something I've been meaning to tell you. I'm not sure what to do about it."

"Oh?" Monica was taken aback.

"I don't want to get anyone in trouble, know what I mean? But I saw something at that fundraiser you had at the farm."

Now Monica was really intrigued. Teddy began to fuss and she gently pushed the stroller forward and back until he quieted down.

"There was that lady who was dishing out the hot chocolate. The plain one with the mousy brown hair. I thought it was peculiar but at the time it didn't really register. Not until I heard that Winslow had been killed. That was a shock, I can tell you."

"What did you see?" Monica prompted. Her feet were freezing and surely Vale's food was getting cold. She bent over the stroller and made sure the blanket around Teddy was well secured.

"I noticed Winslow go up to get some hot chocolate. And I thought I saw that lady—I don't know her name—put something in his cup."

Monica tried to mask her indrawn breath. "Have you told the police?"

"No. That's what I wanted to talk to you about. I don't want to bother them if this is totally irrelevant. I bet they get false leads all the time."

Monica was already shaking her head. "You should definitely tell the police about it. Ask for Detective Stevens. She's handling the case."

Vale doffed an imaginary hat. "Thanks. I'll do that. As soon as I finish my hamburger." He tapped the bag in his hand. "I'm starving. Nice to see you." He waved and turned to cross the street.

Monica wondered if her mouth was hanging open. He had to have been talking about Sharon Dort. She was the only one doling out the cocoa. Monica had offered to relieve her but she'd insisted she was fine.

Was it because she was planning to spike Winslow's drink with some sort of cough medicine or antihistamine? And if that was the case, was she also the one who finished the job by bashing him on the head?

Chapter 15

Greg was shelving books when Monica walked into Book 'Em. The store was warm and cozy with books piled haphazardly on various surfaces and comfortable chairs scattered about.

"You're a sight for sore eyes," Greg said and bent to kiss Monica. He peered into the stroller. "I think someone's been enjoying the fresh air. Those chubby cheeks of his are so rosy." Greg gestured toward the shopping bag in the stroller's storage basket. "I see you've been to Twilight."

"Teddy and I are doing some Christmas shopping." Monica looked around the store. "I'm thinking about a book for Mick. He says he likes to read to improve his English." She pursed her lips. "But which book?"

"I think your friendly local bookseller might be able to help you there." Greg smiled. "How about the latest Jack Reacher book? It's a big hit. It's been flying off the shelves."

"That sounds perfect. Mick seems like a Jack Reacher sort of guy."

"I'll grab a copy and bring it home so you don't have to carry it with you."

"I thought I'd go to the diner and get you some dinner. Have you eaten?"

"No. I haven't been able to leave the store. I'd love a meatball sandwich and some fries."

"By the way, I take it there's been no news from Wilma?"

"Nope. Not a peep." Greg ran his hand through his hair.

"We have her address. Maybe the neighbors know something. They saw her leave with a suitcase or she asked them to water her plants."

"I suppose it's possible. But it seems like a waste of time to me. I called Stevens with the address and she said she was sending a team around to check Wilma's house."

Monica didn't tell Greg, but she planned to visit Wilma's neighborhood first thing in the morning. Whether or not she'd learn something useful remained to be seen.

• • •

The smell of bacon frying lingered in the kitchen as Monica fed Teddy. Greg was in his jacket ready to leave for the store and Nancy was on her way to babysit. Monica fibbed that she was going Christmas shopping at the mall in Grand Rapids. She felt a twinge of conscience about lying to Greg but she knew he'd worry if she told him where she was really going.

Greg had given her Wilma's address and Monica had it tucked in her pocket. She was waiting in the kitchen with Teddy asleep in his carry cot when Nancy arrived. Monica had brewed a pot of tea for her mother and put out some cranberry muffins.

As soon as Nancy was settled, she headed out. She had told her the same lie she'd told Greg—that she was going Christmas shopping. A thought occurred to her as she was pulling out of the driveway: wouldn't they expect her to return home with some shopping bags? She should have thought of that earlier. Hopefully a solution would come to her on the way home.

Wilma lived in an older house nestled in a row of equally old houses. Huge shade trees, their branches stripped bare of leaves, formed a canopy over the rooftops. Wilma's house needed a touch-up of paint here and there but was otherwise in decent repair.

Monica was pleased to see there were lights on in the neighboring houses. Hopefully that meant people were at home.

She walked up the path leading to the house to the left of Wilma's. The slate was covered with patches of ice and Monica had to step carefully. She almost fell a few times but managed to regain her balance. A branch from an overgrown bush by the front door snagged her pants and she had to wrestle herself free of its clutches.

Taking a deep breath to steady herself, she rang the bell and waited, hoping someone would answer. Suddenly the door was flung open, taking her by surprise.

"Yes? Whatever you're selling, we don't want it." The woman looked to be in her late thirties, with dyed black hair pinned up haphazardly and an unlit cigarette dangling from her lips.

"I hope you can help me. I'm looking for my friend Wilma." Monica gestured in the direction of Wilma's house. "She lives next door. I haven't heard from her in days. She's not answering her phone and I'm worried."

The woman hesitated for a moment. "Come on in. It's beastly cold out there." She wrapped her arms around herself.

Monica stepped inside and was hit by a wall of heat. No wonder. The woman was wearing a cropped tank top and a pair of ripped denim shorts. She would hate to see her heating bill. She followed the woman into the kitchen. A man was standing at the sink, leaning over it, eating a slice of pizza. He glanced at Monica, downed the last bite of his meal and left the room without a word.

"Don't mind him. He's my younger brother. Buddy comes by occasionally for a taste of civilization and a home-cooked meal. He's the caretaker for a bunch of cabins at a campground up north." She rolled her eyes. "They're pretty primitive. Not my cup of tea but at least it gives him a roof over his head.

"I'm Zoe, by the way." She put the unlit cigarette down on the table. "I'm trying to quit smoking." She screwed up her face. "Going cold turkey. Expensive habit, you know?"

Monica had never smoked but she'd seen the prices on cartons of cigarettes at the drugstore checkout counter. Zoe wasn't kidding. It was an expensive habit.

"Do you know Wilma well?"

Zoe shrugged. Her shoulders poked through the thin fabric of her top. "I don't know that you'd say we know each other well. My parents left me this house so we've been neighbors for a long time. We used to play together as kids, with my younger brother and the boy who used to live at the end of the street. I've forgotten his name. They moved a long time ago. We'd run around the backyards playing tag until it got too dark to see. But as we grew up, we saw less and less of each other. By then we didn't have much in common, you know what I mean?"

"I don't suppose you know where she's gone? We're worried about her."

"Sorry. I don't have a clue."

Monica was disappointed but there was still the house on the other side of Wilma's. She was grateful to get outside. After Zoe's overheated house, it no longer seemed so cold and she relished the feel of the fresh air on her face.

She picked her way along the ice-covered sidewalk, past Wilma's house, to the one on the other side of her. Someone had strewn salt on the walkway and it was blessedly free of ice.

Monica paused in front of the neighbor's door. A wreath of pine branches studded with shiny ornaments hung above the old-fashioned door knocker. She rang the bell. She was about to turn away when the door opened.

"Yes?" An older woman peered at Monica through thick glasses. Her abundant gray hair was neatly coiled into a bun and she was wearing what Monica's grandmother would have called her Sunday best. "Can I help you, dear?" She looked at Monica quizzically.

"I hope so. I'm worried about my friend Wilma who lives next door to you. Do you know her?"

"Of course I do, dear. We've lived next door to each other for oh, I don't know how long now. Since she was in pigtails." She held the door wider. "Why don't you come in and get warm? I could make us a cup of tea."

"Thank you." Monica stepped into the foyer. It was warm but not nearly as stifling as Zoe's house had been.

"I'm Edna, and you are?"

"Monica. Monica Albertson."

"Pleased to meet you, Monica. Why don't you sit down while I make some tea." She gestured toward the small parlor.

"There's really no need to bother —"

"It's no trouble at all. I won't be a minute."

Monica took a seat in the living room and looked around. Lace curtains framed the bay window with a flowered valance hanging above. The furniture was old-fashioned but the paintings on the wall were decidedly not. Monica studied the one with blocks of red and yellow color. It reminded her of the Rothko paintings she'd seen in the Chicago art museum.

Moments later, Edna came in carrying two steaming mugs of tea. She placed one in front of Monica and placed her own on the side table next to her chair.

"How do you like my paintings?" Her eyes twinkled behind her glasses.

"I was just admiring them."

"My son did them. He's a very talented artist." She smiled. "And a wonderful son. He's good to me." She reached for her mug of tea. "You said you're friends with Wilma?"

"Yes. She's been working at Book 'Em, my husband's bookstore, for several years."

Edna's face lit up. "She thinks the world of your husband. It's Greg, isn't it?"

Monica nodded. "She hasn't shown up for work and she's not answering her phone. We're worried. It's not like her. She's always been so reliable." Monica wrapped her hands around her mug of tea. "Have you seen her or heard from her?"

Edna frowned. "Let me see. Now that you mention it, I haven't seen Wilma for over a week."

"Is that unusual?"

"Yes. Every couple of days she'd stop by for a chat and a cup of tea. It was very kind of her. I do get lonely sometimes, although my son visits as often as he can."

"Do you have any idea where she might have gone? To stay with a relative or friend?"

"I'm afraid I don't know. Poor Wilma was just about alone in this world since her mother died. It's very sad. Sandra worked herself to death taking on two jobs so they could keep their house."

Monica's ears perked up. "Oh?"

Edna nodded, rocking back and forth. "The landlord kept raising the rent. After they paid it, they barely had enough money to buy food. I used to slip them a care package now and then. Anonymously because Sandra was proud. She wouldn't take charity. She wouldn't even go to the food pantry when things got tough."

"That's terrible." Not for the first time, Monica vowed to never stop being thankful for all that she and Greg had.

"It was a month before Sandra died when some relative they didn't even know about left her a small inheritance. It made it possible for Wilma to stay on in the house after her mother passed away." Edna gripped the arms of her chair. "Wilma hated that landlord something fierce. A real-life Mr. Potter. She blamed him for her mother's death. I blame him too. He'd come around to collect the rent, showing off in that fancy car of his. Sandra worked herself into an early grave to keep a roof over their heads. I heard he was dead now too. Murdered, if you can believe it." She sniffed. "A fitting end for him."

"Was the landlord killed recently?"

Edna nodded.

Monica doubted there'd been another murder she hadn't heard about. Cranberry Cove was too small to hide news like that. "What was his name? Was it George Winslow, by any chance?"

"Why, yes. That's the one. George Winslow."

Chapter 16

"I wish Wilma would get in touch." Monica had had to come clean about visiting Wilma's neighbors instead of doing Christmas shopping. The lack of shopping bags had given her away.

Greg stirred the pot on the stove. He was making his famous tortilla soup for dinner. "Every time my phone rings, I get my hopes up. I know I sometimes found Wilma's devotion annoying, but I'd give anything to see her walk through the door of the shop tomorrow morning."

"Me, too." Monica wiped Teddy's mouth with a burp cloth. "And in light of Winslow's murder, it seems rather suspect."

Greg whirled around, the spoon in his hand. "You don't seriously think that Wilma did it, do you? Even though that neighbor of hers said she hated him." He shook his head. "I can't picture Wilma bashing someone over the head."

"Of course not. But it might seem that way to the police. Assuming they find her. I'm not sure how hard they're looking."

"Has Stevens said anything . . . ?"

"Not yet. I hope we hear something soon."

• • •

After dinner, when Teddy was in bed and Greg was watching television, Monica got out her laptop and powered it up. She'd been thinking about Vale's comment that he saw Sharon Dort put something in Winslow's drink. She thought of the article in the *Cranberry Cove Chronicle* about the anonymous woman's husband who fell asleep at the wheel and had a fatal accident. It was eerily similar to Sharon's story about her spouse. She was almost positive that Sharon and the anonymous woman were one and the same. How could she find out?

The reporter who wrote the article must have known the woman's name, but Monica also knew they were reluctant to reveal their sources. She drummed her fingers on the kitchen table. What to do? Was it worth a shot anyway? She wouldn't know until she tried.

She searched for the article and brought it up on the screen. There was no byline under the heading. She tried the bottom of the article and once again came up short. She rested her chin in her hands. What now? Was it possible the editor of the paper might remember who wrote the piece?

The *Cranberry Cove Chronicle*'s office wasn't far. She'd stop by tomorrow.

• • •

Monica set out early on Monday. The morning was crisp and clear with cloudless blue skies. She had learned to appreciate the sunny days because in winter, they were few and far between.

The *Chronicle*'s offices were located on the other side of the harbor. She cruised down Beach Hollow Road, where the shops were just beginning to open. Hennie Van Velsen was opening the door of Gumdrops, and as she approached the butcher shop, she noticed Bart switching the sign from *Closed* to *Open*.

The boats that were normally tied up in the marina were now in dry dock and the Cranberry Cove Yacht Club parking lot was empty. On the other side of the harbor, the neighborhood became a bit run-down. She passed the Harborside Lounge Bar and Grill, where the exalted name did nothing to elevate the seediness of the bar inside. In a concession to the holiday season, a tired-looking wreath had been hung on the door, the tails of its silver bow flapping in the wind.

The *Chronicle* had moved to a new location a few miles beyond the harbor. It was a squat cement building with few adornments, although a string of colored lights outlined the door. Monica pulled into the parking lot, which was almost empty, and parked.

The wind grabbed her scarf when she got out of the car and flung the ends across her face. She grabbed them and tucked them inside her coat as she made her way to the *Chronicle* entrance. Lights were on and she hoped that meant someone was already at work.

A man was seated at a desk in the front that had a miniature artificial Christmas tree in one corner. He was huge and made the desk look as if it belonged to a child, his knees barely able to fit underneath it. He startled when he heard the door open.

Monica cleared her throat, which had suddenly become rather dry. No matter how many times she approached someone while searching for clues, the butterflies rampaging in her stomach never quieted down.

"I'm looking for the editor. Is he in?"

The man pushed his chair back and stretched out his legs. "You're looking at him. Dennis O'Grady at your service." He had a nice smile and Monica felt encouraged.

"I know this is an odd question, but I'm trying to find the reporter who wrote an article in the *Chronicle* about George Winslow and WinGeo."

He raised an eyebrow. "Are you doing one of those true crime podcasts on Winslow's murder?"

"Oh, no. Nothing like that." Monica suddenly realized it was going to be hard to explain. "I need to ask him or her a question."

"What's the date of the article?"

Monica pulled a piece of paper out of her pocket and gave Dennis the date.

"Give me a sec." He motioned to the computer on the desk. "My laptop is in my office."

Moments later, he came out cradling an open laptop in his arms. "Is this the article you're looking for?" He turned it so Monica could see the screen.

She read the title of the piece, "Geosinex Taken Off Shelves." "Yes, that's the one. Do you know who wrote it? There's no byline."

Dennis turned the laptop around and tapped the screen with his finger. "That must have been Chuck Morgan. That was his beat."

"Is he in? Can I please speak to him?"

Dennis was already shaking his head. "He retired a couple of years ago."

Monica tried to hide her disappointment. "Do you know where he lives?"

"Yeah. You know that independent retirement community right when you get off the highway? Lifestyle Retirement?"

"I do." Monica had passed it many times on her way back from Grand Rapids.

"That's where you'll find him. Good luck. And merry Christmas," he added as Monica opened the door.

"Merry Christmas," she called over her shoulder.

• • •

Lifestyle Retirement wasn't far. Monica glanced at her watch. Janice, Mick and Nancy would already be at the farm kitchen. Surely, they could carry on without her for a bit longer. They had all been working with her long enough to know what to do.

She plugged the address into her GPS and made a left turn out of the parking lot. She followed the directions and it didn't take long before she saw the sign for the retirement community.

It was a long, low brick building that looked to be about two stories tall. The massive pine tree out front was adorned with lights and had a gilt star at the top. Cars were neatly parked alongside the retaining pond, which had a thin layer of ice on it.

Monica found a space, got out and locked the doors. There appeared to be a main lobby in the center of the building and she hoped someone would be there to help her.

Furniture had been pushed to the sides to accommodate a Christmas tree that dominated the middle of the lobby. It was surrounded by boxes wrapped in shiny gold paper and tied with silver ribbon. A small desk sat in a corner and had a name plate reading *Receptionist* on top. A woman with half-glasses dangling from a chain sat behind it.

She gave Monica a big smile. "Can I help you?"

"I'm here to see Chuck Morgan. Can you tell me what apartment he's in?"

"Chuck Morgan. Is he a relative of yours? Such a nice man. Always holds the door open for the ladies and isn't above helping out now and then. He's one of our younger residents. Quite handsome too."

Monica raised her eyebrows. "His apartment number?"

The woman poked at her computer with one finger. "He's in number ten. It's in that wing." She pointed to Monica's left.

Monica thanked her and headed down the hallway, glancing at every apartment number as she went by. Number ten turned out to be at the very end. She knocked on the door.

It opened almost immediately. "Oh!" Morgan said. "I was just about to go down for my mail." He frowned. "What can I do for you? If you're selling something, I don't want it. Unless it's Girl Scout Cookies, of course." He narrowed his eyes. "But you look a bit too old to be a scout."

The receptionist had been right, Monica thought. Morgan was rather good-looking. He still had a thick head of silver hair, a patrician nose, firm chin and the crinkles around his eyes spoke to a sense of humor.

Monica decided to take a bit of license. "I'm investigating the Winslow murder."

"Winslow, huh? Come on in."

Monica followed him into a small but bright living room with a leather sofa and a recliner facing the television mounted on the wall.

He perched on the arm of the chair. "I have to warn you, I don't know anything about Winslow's murder. Never met the man, although I did cover WinGeo back in the day. What is it you wanted to know?"

Monica had made a copy of the article in question. She handed it to Morgan. "Do you remember the name of the woman who was quoted anonymously?"

Morgan scanned the article. He flicked it with his finger. "I do remember her. I felt so sorry for her. She wanted to sue WinGeo and Winslow but couldn't find a lawyer who would touch it. Too difficult to prove. Besides, no one wanted to go up against the high-priced legal firepower Winslow could afford to hire."

"You don't happen to remember her name, do you?"

"Strangely enough, I do. For some reason, it's stuck with me all these years. Sharon Dort. Her name was Sharon Dort."

• • •

So, she'd been right, Monica thought as she made her way to Sassamanash Farm. Sharon Dort was the woman who'd been quoted in that *Cranberry Cove Chronicle* article. She obviously had a reason to despise Winslow and Vale had seen her put something in Winslow's drink. It had to have been the antihistamine they'd found in his blood. Had it made him drowsy enough for her to hit him over the head?

She put it out of her mind as she opened the door to the farm kitchen. The sound of the mixer whirring and the thump of Mick's rolling pin filled the air. "Hello," she called out.

"She started it," Nancy said as soon as Monica walked in and before she even had time to take off her jacket. Nancy pointed at

Janice and glowered.

"I did not." Janice all but stamped her foot.

"Please tell me you're not arguing about politics?" Monica looked at Mick, who shrugged his shoulders.

"She"—Nancy glared at Janice—"thinks you should start potty training a child at two years old. I told her that was too young."

"Too young?" Janice spat. She folded her arms across her chest. "Would you have the child going to school in diapers? My mother had all five of us out of diapers shortly after our second birthday."

"Of course not. But they may not be ready at such an early age. Children mature at different rates. If you wait a bit longer, your job will be a lot easier."

Monica held up a hand. "Enough. You're both entitled to your opinions but I will decide when Teddy needs to be toilet trained in consultation with his pediatrician." Monica lowered her voice. "Now, let's get to work. Nora will need product for the afternoon crowd."

Soon the oven was full with trays of cookies baking and everyone was busy with their own tasks, Janice whipping up batter for coffee cakes and Nancy rolling out dough for scones, and although Nancy and Janice occasionally shot dirty looks at each other, relative peace had settled. At least for the moment.

Monica worked for the rest of the morning, stirring compote in a pot on the stove and chopping peppers for cranberry salsa. She took a break at noon to eat her sandwich and then began working on the dough for cranberry bread.

She'd finished the last batch when she glanced at the clock and pulled off her apron. "I have a dental appointment so I'm off."

"Do you have a toothache?" Nancy said.

"No. It's only a routine cleaning."

At least she hoped so, Monica thought as she drove toward downtown. She knew she wasn't alone in her sentiment, but she didn't particularly enjoy visits to the dentist. Especially a new one. She was only doing this in hopes of gaining a nugget or two of information about Debra Winslow's relationship with Owen Evans.

The familiar smell greeted her as soon as she stepped off the elevator on the third floor. She opened the door to the waiting room and looked around. A lone woman was seated next to a large potted plant flipping the pages of a magazine. She was jiggling her foot up and down. Was she nervous? Monica wondered. Or was it simply a habit?

The receptionist greeted her and told her to have a seat. Monica fiddled with the strap of her purse as she waited. Finally, a young woman in scrubs and with a mask dangling below her chin walked into the room and called her name.

Monica followed her to one of the examining rooms and settled into the chair. It was surprisingly comfortable. If nothing else, this was giving her a chance to get off her feet for a bit. The hygienist opened several drawers in a metal cabinet, then turned to Monica. "I'll be right back."

Monica heard her talking to someone in the hallway. She didn't pay much attention until Debra Winslow's name caught her ear. The two women were gossiping about their boss and Debra.

"I heard him say he's head over heels," one of them reported.

"And now her husband is dead," the other hygienist said.

"Quite convenient, don't you think. I heard her talking with Dr. Evans and she was worried that her husband was beginning to suspect something. She was afraid she wouldn't get any money if he divorced her."

"All set," the hygienist sang out and Monica jumped. She'd been so intent on eavesdropping on the conversation she hadn't heard her come in.

"Let's see what we have here," she said as Monica opened her mouth.

Monica barely registered what was going on. She was mentally evaluating all the suspects in Winslow's murder. She'd ruled out Emery but there were still a number of others to consider. Thank heavens it wasn't up to her to unravel this puzzle. It was only her stubborn curiosity that kept her going.

• • •

Monica was leaving the dentist's office when her cell phone rang. It was Greg. The poor man was starving and he hoped Monica could pick up something for him at the diner. Monica had offered to make him a sandwich that morning but he'd been in too much of a hurry, pecking her on the cheek and dashing out the door.

The diner was buzzing with customers having dinner. Many were farmers and their day started early and ended early. The waitress whizzed up and down with trays burdened with platters of creamed turkey on toast and meat loaf and mashed potatoes. The smell of hot oil and grilling meat hung in the air.

Monica pulled out her phone as she waited in line for take-out. Despite her having raised an eyebrow, Greg had insisted on having a hot pastrami sandwich with an order of fries and had promised to begin watching his cholesterol at their very next meal.

The door opened, letting in a cold breeze, but in the heat of the diner it was more than welcome. Perspiration glistened on Gus's forehead and one of the servers waiting for her order fanned herself with a napkin. The door opened and closed several more times. The booths were all full, as were the stools at the counter, and the take-out line was growing.

Monica looked behind her and was surprised to see Emery waiting. He was talking to a woman behind him. Did he know her or had he struck up a conversation with a stranger? The woman moved and Monica was able to see her face. It was Chelsea. Their conversation was animated, judging by their hand gestures, and Chelsea's face was tinted slightly pink. Her expression was the most joyful Monica had ever seen it. A budding attraction? she wondered.

Her mother often accused her of being a hopeless romantic ever since Greg had entered her life. Maybe so, but she couldn't help but wish the same good fortune for Chelsea.

Then it was her turn. She ordered Greg's sandwich and Gus gave her a slight smile, so slight she almost missed it, as she stepped away from the counter. Several minutes later she was holding a paper bag emitting delicious aromas. She inhaled deeply. She was tempted to eat the sandwich herself.

Greg was waiting on a customer who had laid a stack of books on the counter when Monica walked into Book 'Em. He looked harried and Monica could tell he'd run his hands through his hair more than once. She signaled to him that she was leaving his sandwich in the storeroom. She hoped he'd have a chance to eat it while it was still hot, but she supposed a cold sandwich was better than no sandwich at all.

She waved goodbye and glanced across the street as the door shut behind her. Workmen in overalls were doing something in front of Bijoux. She looked at her watch. She had just enough time to check out what progress Estelle was making.

As she crossed the street, she realized she had become as nosy as the other residents of Cranberry Cove and she had to laugh at herself. In a small town, you found amusement where you could.

A ladder was propped against the building, along with a large brand-new sign. Monica had to turn her head sideways to read the writing. *Estelle's* was splashed across the board in curly white script set against a hot pink background. She was peering in the window when the door opened and Estelle appeared.

"What do you think?" She gestured toward the sign. "I wanted something that would stand out."

It was going to stand out, all right. "It's very . . . bright."

"I'm having the walls inside painted that same pink, with white trim."

Monica shuddered. It was going to be like walking into a cloying sea of cotton candy.

"For the window display, I've ordered these wonderful jewelry stands. They look like hands with the palm up and I'll hang the necklaces from their fingers and place the other pieces in their palms." Monica was trying to picture that when Estelle's cell phone rang. "I've got to take this." She went back inside.

Monica noticed that Estelle's nails were painted the same pink as the background of the sign and matched the velour top she was wearing with her black leggings.

She waved goodbye through the window and was about to start down the street when she noticed Jason Vale headed in her direction. His step was brisk and his arms swung rhythmically back and forth at his sides like a metronome.

He waved and began to walk faster. "Monica," he called. He was slightly breathless when he reached her. "How are you?" There was a smudge of white paint along his jawline.

"Fine. How is your store coming along?"

He grinned. "Almost done. I've started planning my grand opening." He pushed up his sleeve and scratched at an angry-looking red spot on his arm.

Monica eyed it. "Should you see a doctor about that?"

"Nah. It's just some kind of bug bite. I've been applying tea tree oil and it's getting better." He pushed his sleeve back down. "I'm going to announce the opening in the *Cranberry Cove Chronicle* and I'm also setting up some social media. I hope you'll come."

"Of course."

"Speaking of newspapers, I haven't seen anything recently about the murder at the fundraiser, have you?"

Monica hesitated. "No, I haven't." Vale had a very open face and she was almost tempted to confess some of the things she'd discovered, but something stopped her. She might be jumping to conclusions and she certainly didn't want to spread false rumors. She had no illusions about how quickly and how far the information would spread.

"It's been great seeing you. I'd better get going. The cabinets are supposed to be delivered any moment now."

Monica crossed the street to her car. She was lost in thought when a man in a pickup truck beeped at her. She scurried across the road to the safety of the sidewalk. Something was niggling at her but she couldn't put her finger on it. Was it something to do with Estelle and her shop or had Vale said something that had rung a bell? It was so frustrating and she hoped it would come to her later.

Chapter 17

Monica's cell phone rang early Tuesday morning. She recognized Alice's number. "Monica. I'm afraid I won't be able to make it today. I've put my back out and the doctor has me lying down with ice packs at least for the day. I hope you can manage. I should be back on my feet tomorrow. I know it's bothersome." She laughed. "For both of us."

"We'll be fine," Monica said as her spirits fell. She had no illusions about back injuries. Her mother had put hers out once and she was laid up for over a week.

"Well, Teddy," she said after she'd hung up. "It's just you and me today. And Grandma, Janice and Mick."

She was driving to the farm when she realized she'd forgotten to eat breakfast. No matter. She'd nibble on some cranberry goodies when she got there.

You'd think a celebrity—an actor or a musician—had arrived at the farm kitchen the way everyone greeted Teddy's appearance.

"He's grown," Janice said as she peered into Teddy's carry cot.

"He's Grandma's little darling, aren't you." Nancy reached down and tickled his tummy.

Monica needn't have worried that Teddy was going to be neglected while she worked. Even Mick took a turn holding him when he began to fuss.

"You're a natural," Monica said as she watched him.

"I do hope to have children someday." He smiled. "But first I have to find my bride."

Mick's rather precipitous first marriage had ended when his new wife was murdered. It had been a horrifying experience and Monica hoped he would soon be ready to move on.

She began mixing up the batter for a batch of oatmeal cookies with cranberry-orange filling. She still hadn't called Stevens to tell her about Sharon Dort and what Vale had seen at the fundraiser, and she wasn't so sure Vale intended to tell her himself. She would ring her as soon as she got this first load of cookies into the oven.

Monica had put two trays of cookies into the oven when her cell phone rang. She was shocked to discover it was Sharon Dort. Was it telepathy?

"I got your number from Chelsea. I hope you don't mind me calling you," Sharon said in a shaky voice.

Monica's curiosity was piqued. What could Sharon want to speak to her about? Her conscience nagged at her. She still hadn't told Stevens about Sharon doctoring Winslow's hot chocolate. Assuming Vale was right about it. But what reason would he have for making it up?

"I have to talk to you. Can you meet me somewhere?"

"I can come by the animal shelter."

Sharon hesitated. "I'd rather not meet here. Can we meet somewhere else?"

Monica's stomach rumbled and that gave her an idea. "How about we meet at the Cranberry Cove Inn for brunch. My treat."

Her remark was met with stunned silence. Finally, Sharon spoke. "If you're sure."

"Yes. Meet me in half an hour."

• • •

The Cranberry Cove Inn was quiet. Weekdays in the off-season generally were, although business picked up on the weekends with the trickle of tourists who came to Cranberry Cove to enjoy its quaint downtown.

A Christmas tree, rather sedately decorated with red, green and gold ornaments, stood blinking in the lobby. A sweeping staircase, the railing wound with an evergreen garland tied with red bows, led to the second floor.

Sharon was waiting for Monica when Monica arrived. She looked nervous and Monica couldn't tell if it was because of what she intended to say or whether she felt out of place in the Inn's lobby.

The restaurant was located behind the lobby. The large windows, which were adorned with wreaths and large gold bows, afforded sweeping views of Lake Michigan.

A subdued buzz filled the room, where most of the patrons were businessmen in suits. The hostess led Monica and Sharon to a table in a quiet corner and placed menus in front of them. Sharon seemed ill at ease, cradling her purse in her lap.

A server buzzed by their table, order pad at the ready. "Have you decided?"

Monica handed her the menu. "I'll have the eggs Benedict, please."

The server tilted her head at Sharon. "And you?"

Sharon glanced at the menu frantically. "The French toast, please." Her voice was so soft the server had to ask her to repeat it twice.

"The police came to see me," Sharon blurted out as soon as the server was out of earshot.

Monica was startled. Perhaps Vale had called Stevens after all.

Sharon's hands trembled slightly as she picked up her napkin. "I don't know what to do. I didn't have anything to do with George Winslow's death. I'm afraid they don't believe me."

"What did they say?"

"Someone saw me put something in Winslow's hot cocoa."

"Is it true?"

The server came by with a pot of coffee and filled their cups. Sharon waited until she was a safe distance away to answer.

"It's true," she said, looking down at her lap.

"But . . . why? What was the stuff you put in his drink?"

"It was cough syrup. The same kind that killed my husband. Geosinex. I'd saved the rest of the bottle."

"The cough syrup didn't kill your husband. He had a car accident."

Sharon's head shot up. "Yes, because the cough syrup made him so drowsy, he fell asleep at the wheel of his car. If there'd been a warning label on the bottle, he never would have gone out that morning. My Albert was a cautious man. He followed the rules. He would never have taken the car out if he'd known."

Their meals had arrived and while Monica was devouring hers. Sharon was merely picking at her French toast, cutting off pieces and moving them around on her plate.

"Were you trying to kill Winslow? Hoping the same thing would happen to him?" Monica kept her voice low. Things had suddenly become more complicated. Would what Sharon did be considered attempted murder? Monica didn't for a minute believe that Sharon had been the one to hit Winslow over the head.

Sharon's face turned as white as the tablecloth. "No. No, of course not. I would never do that."

Monica paused with her fork in the air. "But . . . why then?"

"I only wanted to embarrass him. He acts so high and mighty, I thought I'd knock him off his high horse. He takes a car and driver everywhere so I knew there was no chance that he'd be getting behind the wheel. Someone else might have been hurt and I would never want that." She picked up her coffee cup with both hands and brought it to her mouth. "I'm not a bad person." She looked at Monica with wide eyes.

"Then what did you hope to accomplish by giving him the cough syrup?"

"I thought I'd give him a dose of his own medicine. I figured the cough syrup would make him woozy and he'd stumble around looking as if he was drunk. The revered George Winslow getting drunk at a family fundraiser. What would people think of him then?"

She fixed Monica with an intense stare. "But I didn't hit him over the head. Someone else did that."

• • •

Monica looked at her watch as she got into her car. She'd been away longer than she'd intended. She was lucky to have such a good crew. She knew she could count on them.

The skies began to darken as she drove toward the farm and drivers were turning on their headlights. Bloated clouds hung low in the sky and Monica expected it to start snowing at any minute.

She got to the farm kitchen just before the noon whistle blew. The door was propped open and she quickened her pace. What on earth? As soon as she reached the entrance, she smelled smoke. "Teddy," she screamed frantically. She yanked the door open and looked around. "Where's Teddy?" Her heartbeat slowed a bit when she realized there weren't any flames, although the smoke clouded the air and made her cough. "What's happened? Where's Teddy?"

Nancy, Janice and Mick were fanning the air with towels. They stopped abruptly. "We put Teddy in the storeroom temporarily. There's no smoke in there," Nancy said soothingly. "Everything is under control."

"It doesn't look like it. What happened?" Monica repeated. It was then that she noticed the sheet of burnt scones on the counter. "Oh."

"Somebody forgot to check on the scones." Mick glared at Janice.

"Don't look at me. They were your scones," Janice shot back. Her face crumpled and she looked as if she was about to cry.

"But you said you'd keep an eye on them." Mick glowered at Janice.

Nancy clapped her hands. "Take a deep breath, everyone."

Mick ripped off his apron, threw it on the counter and stormed out.

"It's only some burnt scones," Monica said. "It's really nothing to get so upset about. We can make another batch."

Nancy glanced toward the door. "He won't be out there long. It's freezing and looks like it's about to snow."

Monica shook her head. "That's not like Mick. He's normally so easygoing."

"I think he's worried." Janice picked up the cookie sheet and dumped the scones in the trash. "Remember he said his mother was having surgery?"

Nancy brushed some crumbs off the counter and into her palm. "I know he's frustrated because he can't be there. I gather his father isn't taking it well."

Monica stared at the door Mick had just slammed behind him. He was coming back, wasn't he? She knew he'd return for his coat, but what if he decided to quit and go home to Greece to take care of his parents? What would she do then?

Mick did return eventually, shivering from the cold, his face and hands bright red from the frigid temperatures. He started back to work but was uncharacteristically quiet, his usual smile replaced by a scowl. Nonetheless, Monica couldn't stifle her feeling of unease that Mick might leave for good.

• • •

Monica was feeding Teddy when Greg got home. The look on his face gave Monica her second panic attack of the day. "What's wrong?"

Greg's brows were drawn together and his jaw was clamped tight. He fumbled in the pocket of his coat and pulled out a piece of paper. He handed it to Monica.

It was an ordinary sheet of paper with a message in crude lettering. Monica read it and gasped. "What is this?" She held the paper up.

"What does it look like?" Greg shrugged off his coat.

"It looks like a ransom note." Monica read the text again. Was she dreaming? "Whoever this is"—she waved the piece of paper—"is asking five hundred dollars to return Wilma? But why only five hundred dollars? I thought kidnappers usually wanted bags of money." She frowned. "Where did this come from?"

"It came in the afternoon mail. I saved the envelope but there's no return address and the postage mark is smudged."

Monica felt the blood drain from her face. "Poor Wilma has been kidnapped." She put the note on the kitchen table. "We have to call Stevens."

"Maybe they can get some fingerprints from the paper. We probably shouldn't touch it anymore."

Monica got out her cell phone and quickly clicked on Stevens's number.

"Monica," Stevens said when she answered. "You should put me on speed dial." She laughed but then her voice turned serious. "What's up?"

Monica explained about the ransom note Greg had received.

"I'll be right there." Without saying goodbye, Stevens hung up.

Ten minutes later, the doorbell rang. Stevens stood outside, stamping her feet to get the snow off her boots.

"It's snowing again," she said as she stepped into Monica's foyer. She looked around. "Where is this ransom note?"

"In the kitchen." Monica led her through the family room and into the kitchen, where the note was still spread out on the table.

"So Wilma's gone from just being missing to being kidnapped. My team followed the usual missing persons protocol, including interviewing her neighbors, and came up empty-handed but this is different." Stevens stared at the note. "Rather primitive, isn't it? But I suppose that's the point. A kidnapper is hardly likely to be a Rhodes Scholar. Although you never know. Stranger things have happened." She looked at Greg. "You got this in the mail?"

"Yes. It came this afternoon."

"I remember you said Wilma doesn't have any family or friends that you know of. I wonder if that's why the kidnapper sent this note to you?"

Greg frowned. "I don't know."

Stevens drummed her fingers on the table. "Could it be a joke? Maybe Wilma is playing you?"

Greg all but reared back. "No. Never. Wilma's not like that."

Stevens pursed her lips. "You're probably right." She stared at the note. "I'll get on this right away. I just hope she isn't in any danger."

Chapter 18

Monica barely slept that night. She tossed and turned until Greg finally asked her if she was okay. The truth was, she was worrying about Wilma. Stevens had told them to not even think about paying the ransom but to let the police handle things. That was good since their budget was already stretched tight enough as it was.

But if Wilma was kidnapped, then she must be innocent of Winslow's murder. She hadn't fled because she was afraid of being a suspect, as they'd feared. Monica couldn't believe she'd even thought for a minute that Wilma might be guilty. The very idea was too ridiculous to fathom.

The one bright spot was that Mick was already at the farm kitchen when she got there in the morning. He was slightly bleary-eyed, and had started work on that morning's baking. He greeted her with a smile and was whistling under his breath so he was obviously almost back to his usual self.

She certainly had enough to worry about—Wilma having been kidnapped and Jeff threatening to sell the farm. He said he would talk to Lauren, but had he? She'd have to remind him. A thought froze her in her tracks. Maybe he already had talked to Lauren and was trying to find a way to tell Monica that Sassamanash Farm was going up for sale?

Monica tried to focus on the bread she was kneading and soon the familiar motion began to soothe her. Nancy had started to load the finished product onto the cart to be taken down to the farm store. Monica looked over the selection.

"I think we have enough for now. I'll take it. I could use some fresh air." She reached for her jacket and shoved her arm into the sleeve. It pushed the sleeve of her sweater up to her elbow and she had to wrestle it back into place.

Finally, she was ready. She wheeled the cart out the door and began down the path to the store. It was slow going even though Jeff had cleared off the snow. The ruts were frozen in place and it took some muscle to get the cart over them.

Monica passed the bogs, where the sun glinted off the ice covering. She missed the joyful red of the berries bobbing in the water during the harvest and the pink flowers in the summer.

Jeff had outlined the store with white lights and a small Christmas tree stood blinking in the window. Monica was about to open the door when Jeff appeared around the corner. He had a knit cap pulled down low over his forehead and his hands were stuffed in his pockets.

"Hey, sis. I was just coming to see you."

Monica's breath caught in her throat. Had Jeff spoken with Lauren? Was it good news or bad? She studied his face for clues but couldn't decipher his expression.

"I talked to Lauren last night."

"Oh." Monica's stomach clenched. "What did she say?"

Jeff broke into a grin. "She said she's perfectly happy here on the farm. She loves that she can work remotely and still enjoy the outdoors." He scratched behind his neck. "Here, I thought she was longing for Chicago and the city life, but apparently not. I guess I shouldn't jump to conclusions." He looked slightly sheepish.

Monica felt almost lightheaded with relief. She put a hand on the cart to steady herself.

"You okay, sis?"

"Yes. I'm fine. Really fine." Her breath sent clouds of vapor into the air. "But my toes are getting numb so why don't we go inside?" She gestured toward the door of the store, where a wreath hung in the middle of the window.

"I've got some stuff to do." Jeff jerked a thumb over his shoulder. "I've got a couple of repairs to make on the sander and I need to take a look at the truck."

"Go on." Monica made a shooing motion. "And say hello to Lauren for me."

She felt her shoulders relax as she watched Jeff make his way across the field toward the barn. Everything was going to be okay. At least as far as the farm was concerned.

• • •

Monica was bushed by the end of the day. Her back hurt and her feet ached. All she wanted to do was curl up on the sofa with Teddy. She put on her jacket and reached into her pocket. A piece of paper came out with her glove and fell on the floor. An old grocery list, she thought as she picked it up. A quick glance told her it was her Christmas shopping list, and not very many names were checked off. Instead of curling up on the couch, she needed to go shopping or she'd never be ready for Christmas.

Alice had her coat, hat and gloves already laid out on a chair when Monica got home.

She slipped on her coat and did up the buttons. "Teddy has been quite content in his carry cot but I suspect he's going to need a change very soon. I would do it but I'm afraid I have to scoot. A friend and I are going to the mall in Grand Rapids to do some Christmas shopping." She pulled on a knit cap and the pompom on top wobbled.

And that's what she needed to do too. "Looks like we're going for a stroll downtown again, Teddy." Teddy kicked his feet and blew a giant bubble that made Monica laugh.

Once Teddy was fed, changed and secure in his car seat, Monica headed downtown. Once again, the sidewalks were crowded and parking was sparse. She was lucky to get a space when a large SUV pulled out of one.

She bundled Teddy into his stroller, adjusted his hat, which had slipped down, and tucked a blanket around him. They hadn't gone far when they heard singing in the distance. Monica paused to listen. A group of people were singing "O Come, All Ye Faithful," their voices mingling in perfect harmony. The crowds parted and Monica saw the carolers. They were all wearing Santa hats and were carrying an electric candle. People paused as they went by and several briefly joined in, one of them sporting a rich baritone.

Monica had been feeling tired and down but her spirits lifted instantly and she continued briskly down the street, humming to herself.

She wheeled Teddy along the sidewalk, stopping occasionally to peer in a window. She was headed to Danielle's, where she hoped she would find a reasonably priced scarf for her mother, although Danielle's and reasonably priced weren't words you normally heard spoken together.

Quite a number of people were browsing the racks in Danielle's and going through stacks of sweaters. Danielle, a petite French woman who oozed style and sophistication, was behind the counter ringing up sales.

It was difficult maneuvering Teddy's stroller through the small space and Monica breathed a sigh of relief when she reached the scarf display without knocking anything over. She was thrilled to notice a sale sign on the wall above the shelf.

All the scarves were beautiful and it was hard to choose but, in the end, she settled on a lovely one in shades of blue that she thought would match her mother's eyes. She also chose a brightly colored one for Gina. Two gifts down, she thought as Danielle rang up the sale.

She was leaving the store when she noticed the lights on in Bijoux across the street. She waited for a stream of cars to pass then dashed across with Teddy.

Estelle saw her coming and opened the door, beckoning to her. "Come in and get warm." Monica wheeled the stroller into the store. Estelle bent over Teddy with a smile on her face. "He gets more adorable each time I see him. Look at that dimple in his chin. Adorable." She stood up, putting a hand to her back. "I have some coffee going in the back. I just put it on. Would you like some?"

A warm cup of coffee sounded very good to Monica. She could use the jolt of caffeine and the warm cup would feel good in her chilled hands. "Yes, thanks."

Estelle was about to head to the stockroom when the door handle rattled frantically and a woman began banging on the door.

Estelle tsk-tsked and walked toward the door. She opened it a crack and stuck her head out. "I'm sorry, we're not open."

The woman's voice was commanding. "I need to speak with you. Now."

Estelle sighed and opened the door. "How can I help you?"

"I hope you can." The woman stormed into the store and Monica recognized her as Debra Winslow. She half expected Debra to remember her but all her attention was focused on Estelle and she barely glanced at Monica. She didn't seem to notice that all the jewelry cases and display stands were empty and only half the walls had been painted.

"I need to return this." She slammed a box down on the counter.

"I'm sorry but—"

"I found it in my husband's drawer when I was cleaning out his things — such a chore — and I know he didn't buy it for me." Her voice dripped with bitterness. "It's for his mistress. I knew there was someone else and this confirms it. I need you to take it back. It's not something I would ever consider wearing."

"I can understand that." Estelle tapped the lid of the box where Bijoux was written in fancy script. "But this is no longer Bijoux. They sold it and it's mine now. Estelle's."

"Does this mean you can't help me?" Debra's face was a mask of fury. Without another word, she turned on her heel and stomped out of the store, slamming the door behind her.

Estelle shook her head. "What on earth was that all about?"

Monica thought she knew. Winslow had been seeing someone else and Debra knew it. That gave her an even stronger motive to murder him. If he'd traded her in for a new model, what would that have done to her settlement?

• • •

"You look quite spiffy," Alice said when she arrived Thursday morning. "Where are you off to?"

Monica looked down at her black pants and pale green blouse. "You think this is okay? I don't have a lot of need for professional-looking clothes."

"You look fine." Alice patted Monica's arm. "But what's the occasion? A Christmas luncheon?"

"No. Strictly business." Monica reached down to scratch Hercule, who was hovering by her legs. "I'm meeting a buyer from a huge gourmet store in Chicago. It was started by three chefs. Maybe you've heard of it? Cucina Italiana."

"I'm sorry, no. But I'm not all that up on what's new these days. I used to love to go to Chicago to walk the Magnificent Mile checking out all the stores and then for lunch somewhere, but now the thought alone makes me tired." She slapped her thighs with her palms. "I'm quite content staying close to home."

"They're considering carrying our cranberry salsa. This could be huge for Sassamanash Farm."

"Fingers crossed then."

Monica bent over the carry cot, where Teddy was cooing

contentedly. She kissed him on the forehead.

"Off with you then." Alice bent to pick up Teddy. "Good luck," she called after Monica as Monica headed out the door.

Monica's hands were sweating on the steering wheel even though the weatherman had said it was below freezing outside. She kept telling herself she wasn't nervous, that it was just excitement that was making her heart rate gallop. It had been a long time since she'd had a business meeting and she wasn't sure she was ready for it.

Yes, you are, a little voice whispered in her head. She took a deep breath and tried to focus on the festive Christmas decorations as she drove down Beach Hollow Road. She was meeting David Taylor at the Cranberry Cove Yacht Club. It was bound to be quiet at this time of year.

The cocktail lounge with its nautical décor of ships' wheels, fake anchors and fishing net was empty. Monica entered the dining room, where the hostess was waiting. She explained she was meeting someone and the hostess led her to a table for two in a quiet corner.

The restaurant wasn't busy. Two tables were occupied by men in business suits and the rest were empty.

Monica sat down to wait for Taylor. She glanced at her watch. She was five minutes early. A large window gave a view of the harbor. The boats that would normally be gently bobbing up and down there were all in dry dock and the water looked gray and unwelcoming.

Monica found herself fiddling with the fork on the table, rubbing her fingers over the CCYC engraved on the silver as if it was a worry stone. She sensed activity at the hostess station and looked up.

The hostess was leading a man toward her table. He had a round, pleasant face and sandy blond hair that was hanging over his forehead, giving him a boyish look. He greeted Monica with a huge smile and she felt herself begin to relax.

"You must be Monica." He held out a hand. "Dave Taylor." They shook and he pulled out his chair and plopped into it. "A lovely town you have here. Love the Christmas decorations. I've always wondered what it would be like to live in a small place like this."

"It's a bit like living in a fish bowl but it's very comforting."

They exchanged pleasantries until the server had brought their meals. Monica was too nervous to eat much and had ordered a slice of quiche, while Taylor was downing a cheeseburger and fries. They were pushing their finished plates away when Taylor brought up the subject they'd met to discuss.

Monica clenched her hands in her lap. This could mean so much for the farm. She couldn't mess this up.

Taylor wiped his mouth with his napkin and leaned back in his chair. "So how about it? Do you think Sassa . . . what's the farm called again?"

"Sassamanash. It's the Algonquin word for cranberry."

"I see. Of course. Anyway, word of mouth has certainly spread and a number of people have been asking if we carry your salsa. Apparently, they bought some while they were down here on vacation and they can't get enough of it. Do you think you would like to work with us?"

Would she? Monica tried to stifle the grin that threatened to spread across her face.

"We would definitely be interested." Monica aimed for a cool, calm and collected business-like voice when inside she was shouting for joy.

"Excellent." Taylor grinned and held out his hand. "Now let's talk details."

• • •

Monica left the Cranberry Cove Yacht Club with her head buzzing with excitement. She couldn't wait to tell Jeff about the deal she'd made with Cucina Italiana.

Meanwhile, she felt like celebrating. She'd invite Jeff and Lauren for dinner. Perhaps she'd even pick up a bottle of champagne. She pulled out her cell and clicked on his number. It rang several times before he picked up.

She'd planned on telling him about the deal in person because she wanted to see his reaction, but she couldn't stop herself from blurting it out. As she'd expected, Jeff was thrilled. She told him about dinner, but he was sorry, he and Lauren had other plans. They were meeting an old friend of his who he hadn't seen in years.

Monica felt a bit let down but then decided she'd invite her mother, her stepmother and Estelle. That would certainly make things festive, and she was thrilled when they all accepted the invitation.

What to make for dinner? Perhaps Bart would have a suggestion. She moved her car to a spot along Beach Hollow Road and began to walk to Bart's Butcher.

"Howdy," Bart said when she walked through the door. "What can I do you for?"

"I'm having a small dinner tonight and I'm fresh out of ideas. I was hoping you could help."

"A nice pork roast perhaps?" He patted a piece of meat on the counter. "Simmer it in milk and it will come out real tender and juicy."

"That sounds perfect."

Bart began to wrap up the roast. "I see we have two new shops opening here. They're stirring up a lot of excitement in our little town. We haven't had anything new since the Pepper Pot opened." He pulled a piece of string from the ball on the counter. "An apothecary. Imagine. I don't see that too many folks around here are going to go for that, but you never know."

He tied the string and put the meat on the scale. "And there's that new jewelry shop. Used to be Bee-shoe or something like that. Funny name for a store. Anyway, that woman who bought it, is she related to you somehow? I've seen her hanging around with your stepmother."

"She's Gina's mother-in-law. She's moved here from Florida."

"I figured it was someplace like that since she's got a tan and everyone in Cranberry Cove is as white as an unpainted plaster wall." He put the bundle of meat into a paper bag. "I've seen her talking to the guy who's opened the apothecary. They seem pretty friendly. Like real friendly."

"Oh? She's a little old for him, don't you think?"

"You know what they say, to each his own." Bart handed Monica the bag and her credit card.

Were Estelle and Vale . . . ? she wondered as she left the shop. She'd have to find out what was what tonight.

• • •

By the time Monica slid the last batch of cookies out of the oven and put them on a rack to cool, she was beginning to regret having invited Gina and Estelle to dinner. She was ready to collapse. Hopefully, she'd get a second wind. At least the menu was simple—

pork roast, mashed potatoes and peas. Greg said he'd go to the Golden Scoop and pick up a quart of ice cream for dessert. Monica had made some sugared cranberries that would dress it up nicely.

As soon as she got home and Alice had left, she got out her Dutch oven and put it on the stove. Teddy had already been fed and seemed content in his carry cot while she browned the roast on all sides. She added the milk, salt and pepper, put the lid on slightly ajar and turned the burner on low.

She checked on Teddy but he had fallen asleep, his arms over his head as if he was signaling a touchdown. She ran her hand over his head, feeling the silkiness of his hair. She felt tears forming in her eyes as she marveled at how lucky she was. There was a bit of sadness as well. Teddy wasn't going to be a baby forever and one day would go off on his own.

But that was years and years away, she told herself. And right now, she had a dinner to prepare. She'd almost finished peeling the potatoes when Greg got home. He brandished a paper bag with *The Golden Scoop* scrolled across the front.

"The dessert is here," he said as he opened the freezer. "Whatever you're cooking smells delicious."

Monica paused with the vegetable peeler in her hand. "What flavor did you get?"

"Peppermint bark. They're only selling it during December. I thought it sounded appropriately festive."

"I think I hear a car." Monica wiped her hands on a towel and went to the front door.

"Congratulations." Gina walked in brandishing a bottle of champagne. "Jeff told me the good news." She gave Monica an air kiss on both cheeks.

Estelle was right behind her carrying a bottle of wine. "What a lovely home you have." She slipped off her white fake fur parka and handed it to Greg.

Both Gina and Estelle were dressed for the holidays in sequined tops. Gina's was gold and Estelle's was silver. They reminded Monica of a disco ball. Nancy was true to form in a pair of black pants and a simple silk blouse, although with a nod to the season, the blouse was red.

Greg popped the cork on the champagne while Monica fetched

glasses. They'd have to make do with ordinary wineglasses—she didn't have any flutes and the coupes her grandmother had left her were packed away somewhere.

Champagne was passed around and toasts were made and glasses clinked.

The timer dinged and Monica jumped up. "The roast is ready."

Greg shepherded everyone to the dining table while Monica sliced the pork and dished up the peas and mashed potatoes.

"What a delightful meal." Estelle reached for the platter of pork and the bracelets on her wrist jangled. She sighed. "I'm not much of a cook myself. And now that I'm a widow and my Freddie is gone, may he rest in peace, I figure why should I cook for myself when there are so many restaurants around? Whoever invented Door Dash should get the Nobel prize."

"There isn't a lot of fine dining in Cranberry Cove." Nancy reached for her wineglass. "I hope you won't get bored."

"Nah. My Mickey cooks for me now. And get this, he said that when I move into my own place, he'll stock my freezer with home-cooked meals."

"Speaking of widows, I played bridge with Debra Winslow the other day." Nancy reached for the peas. "She seems to be holding up quite well." She raised an eyebrow. "Of course, she has that fellow Owen to console her." She stabbed a piece of meat. "Not that I approve of that relationship, mind you."

Estelle paused with her fork in the air. "Too soon?"

Nancy shook her head. "No, not that."

"What then?"

Nancy looked uncomfortable. "Apparently, she met Owen before . . . um . . . before her husband passed away. I certainly don't approve but what could I say. It isn't my place to pass judgment."

"I guess she figured she shouldn't put all her eggs in one basket." Estelle wiped her lips, leaving a crimson stain on the napkin.

Nancy stared at her. "But surely, she didn't know that her husband was going to be murdered."

"Not unless she did it." Gina took a sip of wine.

Estelle leaned forward eagerly. "Do you think she did it? Knocked off her husband?"

Nancy sighed. "I should certainly hope not, but I do wonder. She is a good bit older than Owen. That's why she got that eye lift. I don't think she needed to worry. If you ask me, it's her money he's after."

Estelle tapped the table with a long fingernail painted raspberry red. "But maybe her hubby found out about Owen and threatened to divorce her? It seems to me that would give him a good reason to stiff her when it came to the money."

Monica frowned. "But that was her husband's money. According to his ex-wife, Angela, he was downright stingy. I doubt Debra would have had free access to it unless . . ."

Nancy gave an exaggerated shiver. "Enough about the murder. Isn't there something else we can talk about?"

"Have you met the new guy in town?" Estelle looked around the table.

"You mean Jason Vale? The man who's opening the apothecary?"

"Yeah, him. Kinda good-looking, don't you think? Those muscular arms and that head of hair."

Gina put a hand on Estelle's arm. "And about twenty years too young."

Estelle made a face. "I'm not planning on marrying him. I just found him interesting. He told me all about his new shop and said I should try ginger for my heartburn."

"When I spoke to him, he did say that he became an apothecary because he didn't trust the big pharmaceutical companies." Monica got up and began clearing the table.

"Let me help you." Nancy pushed her chair back.

Estelle balled up her napkin and put it beside her plate. "He did say something about a trauma having driven him to become an apothecary."

Monica paused with a stack of dinner plates in her hand. "What sort of trauma?"

"He didn't say. But it obviously affected him deeply."

• • •

When Monica carried Teddy downstairs on Saturday morning, Greg was on his knees in front of the Christmas tree.

He turned his head when he heard Monica. "A strand of lights went out. I'm trying to see if I can fix them, otherwise, I'll have to run to the hardware store for some new ones."

Monica glanced at her watch. "Shouldn't you be heading to the store?"

"Felicity is opening up for me this morning. We're staying open late tonight so I thought I'd take the morning off."

Monica was surprised. That store was Greg's baby and it was months before he even trusted Wilma enough to leave her in charge.

"Are you sure?"

Greg dropped the strand of lights and stood up. "Felicity has turned out to be a whirlwind of organization. Very competent. She's even reorganizing the shelves."

"But half the fun of Book 'Em is finding a treasure where you don't expect it—a first edition of an Agatha Christie or Josephine Tey shelved in with the nonfiction crime books."

Greg grinned. "Don't worry. I'll have the shelves in their usual disarray as soon as Wilma's back and Felicity moves on to her next temp job."

Monica cocked her head. "It sounds like the mailman is here. You take Teddy and I'll go check."

"Are you sure?" Greg reached out his arms for the baby. "The walk might be slippery."

"I'll be fine." Monica pulled on her boots, which were waiting on a mat by the door.

"Aren't you going to wear a jacket?"

"Why bother? It's a short walk to the mailbox."

Monica opened the door and a gust of wind fluttered the newspaper scattered across the coffee table. Halfway to the mailbox she began to regret her decision to forgo a jacket. The wind swirled the snow around her ankles and sent shivers down her spine. By the time she reached the end of the driveway, her teeth were chattering and her face was numb. She grabbed the batch of envelopes from the mailbox and began the walk back to the house.

"Warm out there?" Greg said with a teasing smile. Monica swatted his arm with the stack of envelopes. As soon as she got her boots off, she began to flip through them.

"Anything interesting?" Greg shifted Teddy to his other side.

"No . . ." Monica began. The last piece of mail in the pile was a plain white envelope, the kind you can buy anywhere. Their address was printed in clumsy block letters and there was no return address. "This looks like that other note you got. The one about Wilma." Monica slid her finger under the flap and ripped it open.

She took out a single sheet of paper and scanned the message. "It's another ransom note."

She handed it to Greg and he quickly read it. "I don't like the sound of this—pay up or else. Or else what?"

"I agree. That does sound ominous. We'd better let Stevens know."

Chapter 19

Monica had decided to take the day off. Alice was headed to her niece's wedding in Traverse City, so Monica had to either stay home or take Teddy to the farm kitchen with her. She didn't feel too guilty because it was the perfect opportunity to work on the farm's accounts while Teddy napped. She thought of the deal she'd made with Cucina Italiana. The farm was in fairly good shape but the money from the sale of her salsa would mean a lot less worry about how well the crops were doing. But she'd cautioned Jeff not to rely on it until the ink on the contract was dry, and she'd better take her own advice.

She couldn't stop thinking about poor Wilma. Was she scared? Was she being treated okay? Where on earth could she be? She thought back to Stevens's comment. Was it possible that Wilma herself was sending the ransom notes? But why would she do that? To cover up the fact that she'd fled somewhere because she feared she was a suspect in Winslow's murder?

If only she knew where Wilma was. *Think.* She'd already gone over everything she could think of more than once but none of it had yielded any clues.

Wait a minute. The chat with Zoe. What was it she'd said? Monica scrunched up her forehead, as if that would help her remember.

"Bingo," she shouted, startling Teddy, who began to cry in protest. Monica rocked him in her arms.

It was just a hunch but hopefully it was going to pay off.

Monica debated taking Teddy with her, but when she remembered the cigarette smoke in Zoe's house, she decided against it. Who could she call? She decided to see if Gina could get away from Making Scents for a bit.

She knew Gina's assistants came and went with the regularity of the seasons to the point where Gina barely bothered to learn their names. Hopefully the one in residence at the moment was capable of manning the store by herself.

Gina was thrilled to help out and it wasn't long before Monica heard her car in the driveway.

"Thanks for coming," Monica said as Gina cooed over Teddy. "Who's minding the store?"

"Someone named Stephanie something-or-other. She seems quite responsible."

"So, you think you'll keep her?"

"Probably. She isn't annoying. Yet."

"Teddy has been fed and his diaper's been changed. He should be good until I get back."

"Don't worry about a thing. Go on. Get going." Gina shooed her away.

Monica settled into the driver's seat of her car and turned the key in the ignition. Was she going on a wild-goose chase? There was no guarantee that Zoe would even be home.

The street was quiet and she pulled up to the curb in front of Zoe's house. Lights were on and a car was in the driveway. Fingers crossed Zoe was there.

Monica made her way up the path and rang the doorbell. She heard music inside, something with a heavy bass. Surely, the person listening must be deafened by it. She rang the bell again, keeping her finger on it this time.

The music stopped and the door was flung open, sending a burst of heat into the frigid air.

"Yeah?" Zoe stood in the doorway, once again wearing shorts and a T-shirt. "Oh, it's you. Come on in."

Monica quickly loosened her scarf and unbuttoned her coat as Zoe led her into the kitchen. A cigarette was burning in an ashtray on the kitchen island.

"I'm down to half a pack a day." Zoe picked up the cigarette and took a long draw on it. She turned her head and blew the smoke away from Monica. "Quitting cold turkey wasn't for me. I'm tapering off. If this is about Wilma, I'm afraid I already told you everything I know. You didn't find her, did you?"

"I wanted to ask you something else actually."

"Go ahead. Shoot." Zoe leaned her elbows on the island.

"Your brother Buddy was here last time we talked."

"Yeah? What about it?" Zoe's posture immediately became defensive.

Monica chose her words carefully. "You said he is a caretaker at a campground somewhere up north?"

Zoe tapped her cigarette on the edge of the ashtray. "He is, or at least he was the last time I talked to him. He's not real good at keeping jobs." She rolled her eyes.

"Did Wilma know about this campground?"

Zoe shrugged. "I don't know. Maybe. I remember one year she and her mother went up north to go camping. That was the only vacation they ever took as far as I know. Not that we went on a lot of vacations ourselves, mostly day trips to Lake Michigan to go swimming."

"Does Wilma sometimes talk to Buddy when he's here?"

"Not really. Except if they both go to the mailbox at the same time. I've seen them shooting the breeze for a couple of minutes here and there."

"Do you know the name of the campground? You said there are cabins?"

"That's what Buddy told me. They're pretty rustic from his description. But I don't remember the name."

Monica nearly groaned in frustration. "Will you be talking to your brother at some point soon? Could you ask him?"

Zoe stubbed out her cigarette. "Hang on. He gave me a brochure about the place. In case I ever wanted to go." She looked around the kitchen. "Now where did I put it?" She began opening cupboards and drawers. "I think it's in here."

It was obviously the junk drawer, given the miscellaneous assortment of contents. Zoe dug around underneath the pens, pencils, old batteries and what looked like a jar opener.

"Aha." She pulled out a glossy brochure triumphantly. "Here it is." She put it down on the island.

Monica glanced at the cover, where *De Groot's Campground* was written across the front in large white letters against a background of rustic cabins. She checked the address and was pleased to see it wasn't really that far away.

"You can keep it." Zoe gestured toward the brochure. "I don't need it."

Monica tucked it in her pocket. She might be wasting her time, but somehow she didn't think so.

• • •

"I think I know where Wilma is." Monica and Greg were sitting at the kitchen table leafing through the Sunday paper. The smell of bacon lingered in the air and Hercule was snoozing nearby.

"What? Where?" Greg dropped the section of newspaper he'd been holding. "How do you know?"

"It's only a guess but I'd bet anything I'm right."

"Where?" Greg repeated. "Don't keep me in suspense."

"De Groot's Campground in Newaygo."

"What makes you think that?" Greg's brow was wrinkled.

Monica pushed her plate away and leaned her elbows on the table. "I talked to Zoe, Wilma's next-door neighbor. Wilma and her younger brother Buddy used to play together when they were kids and Buddy and Wilma still chat occasionally. Buddy is the caretaker at De Groot's Campground. Zoe said Wilma and her mother went there one summer. What if that's where Wilma is hiding? Buddy could have let her into one of the cabins easily enough. I'm sure he has a set of master keys since he's supposed to be keeping an eye on the place."

Greg's frown deepened. "But what about the ransom notes? You mean you think Wilma wasn't really kidnapped?"

Monica played with the edge of her napkin. "I don't know. But there's something fishy about the whole situation. No one saw Wilma being abducted. Stevens interviewed a number of people and none of them noticed a thing. And those ransom notes seem so . . . so amateurish."

"True. And the drop-off place for the money — that little library on Willow Street in Newaygo opposite the general store."

"What if we go to the campground ourselves? Poke around?"

Greg was shaking his head even before Monica finished talking. "We don't know for sure she hasn't been kidnapped. And we don't know for sure the kidnapper is as harmless as those ransom notes make him sound."

"I have an idea." Monica reached for her cell phone just as Teddy began to cry.

"I'll get him." Greg pushed back his chair.

Zoe had given Monica her telephone number in case Monica had any more questions. Monica scrolled through her contacts, found it, hit call and waited while the phone rang.

Zoe sounded sleepy when she answered.

"I hope I didn't wake you?"

"Nah. I'm still waiting for my first cup of coffee to brew." She yawned. "Have you heard from Wilma?"

"No. And that's why I'm calling." Monica cleared her throat. Hopefully Zoe wouldn't be offended by what Monica had to say. "I think I may know where Wilma is."

"Rats," Zoe exploded. "Sorry, I just sloshed hot coffee on my hand. Go on."

"I think it's possible that Wilma is hiding at the campground your brother is overseeing. The cabins must be empty this time of year."

"Yeah, I suppose they must be. There's nothing to do up there this time of year, no skiing or snowshoeing. There isn't even a lake to skate on." Monica heard a slurp as Zoe sipped her coffee. "You think my brother gave her a key to one of the cabins?"

"I don't know for sure, but I think it's possible, yes."

"What are you going to do?"

Monica hesitated. "Here's the thing. We've received ransom notes saying that Wilma has been kidnapped."

"Kidnapped?" Zoe's gasp came over the line. "No, wait."

"Is it possible your brother . . . ?"

Zoe began to laugh. "Buddy? Gosh, no. Not for real anyway."

"What do you mean?"

"Buddy will do almost anything to avoid holding down a real job. He's tried every scam in the book in order to dodge actual work. I think this might be one of them. I overheard him once trying to persuade his girlfriend of the moment—I think her name was Shona or something like that—to pretend she'd been kidnapped so he could claim the ransom money." Zoe snorted. "Fortunately, Shona was brighter than she looked and refused. They split up shortly after that."

"Do you think he convinced Wilma to play the victim?"

"I don't know. It's possible he simply took advantage, you know, of the situation. Knowing Wilma was hiding from something and he could make it look like a kidnapping and possibly get a few bucks out of it."

"Thanks, Zoe."

"What are you going to do? You're not going to the police, are you?"

"I haven't decided. I'll let you know."

"Buddy doesn't mean any harm."

"I'm sure." Monica ended the call. She put her phone down on the table.

Greg looked at her. "Are you going to call Stevens now?"

Monica pursed her lips. "Maybe not." She proceeded to tell him about her conversation with Zoe.

Chapter 20

Nancy was more than happy to babysit Teddy for a few hours. "I swear he's grown since I last saw him and that was only a few days ago," she said as soon as she arrived and had doffed her coat. She held out her arms and Monica handed Teddy to her.

"I don't know how long we'll be." Monica grabbed her jacket from the closet and put it on.

"Don't worry about that. I've got all day." Nancy rocked Teddy up and down.

"There are bottles of milk in the refrigerator. They just need to be heated, but be sure to check the temperature before—"

Nancy held up a hand. "You forget. I've done this before. We'll be fine. You two go ahead."

Monica had told her mother that she and Greg were driving out to the country for lunch at an inn they'd read about. They took Greg's Volvo. Despite its squeaks and groans, it was more reliable than Monica's Focus. The skies were crystal clear. There weren't any clouds but a contrail streaked across the horizon. Monica imagined being up in a plane with such a clear view of the landscape below.

It hadn't snowed in a few days and the roads were clear, the blacktop sparkling in the sun. Monica had to remind herself they weren't going on an outing but on a mission that had the potential to be dangerous in spite of all the signs indicating otherwise.

Greg put on his blinker and took exit 89 to M-37N. "Not too much further." He glanced at Monica. "You still sure about this?"

Monica wasn't sure at all but she nodded her head. "Yes."

Soon they were headed down a dirt road. Large trees hung over it and snow still nestled in the ruts. Monica felt her teeth clank together as they went over one bump after another. Finally, they came upon a large wooden sign with *De Groot's Campground* on it in raised letters painted white. A rope ran across the road from one side to the other.

Greg put the car in park, got out and unhooked the rope. "So much for security," he said as he got back in and put the car in gear.

The drive wound around in front of a building made to look like a log cabin. A plaque with the word *Office* on it hung on the door and a carved wooden statue of Paul Bunyan holding an ax aloft stood beside it. Rustic cabins nestled under the trees in the distance. A number was affixed to each one and a wooden picnic table stood outside next to a brick barbecue grill.

"They all look empty," Greg said as he drove past the cabins one by one.

Monica felt defeated. Had she been wrong about where Wilma was hiding? They were nearly to the end of the row of cabins when Monica pointed to one. "Look. There's smoke coming from that chimney. And there are logs piled by the door. Someone is in there."

"You think it might be Wilma?"

"I hope so."

Greg was slowly pulling closer to the cabin when they heard a noise behind them. Monica swiveled around. A man in torn jeans and scuffed work boots riding on an ATV was headed toward them.

"Uh-oh," Greg said, peering into the rearview mirror. "Looks like we have company."

"I think it's Buddy, Zoe's brother. The one I think sent those ransom notes."

"Maybe we should get out of here and leave this to the police?"

Monica put a hand on Greg's arm. "Wait. Not yet. I really don't think he's dangerous."

Greg peered into the mirror again. "He certainly doesn't look like a hardened criminal. But maybe we shouldn't take a chance."

Meanwhile, Buddy had pulled up to the passenger side of the Volvo. Monica rolled down her window.

"Hi. We're friends of your sister Zoe's. She told us about this place. We're looking to rent something next summer. Do you have a brochure and a price list?"

Buddy scratched his head. His cuticles were bitten and his nails were rimmed with dirt. "I might have. They'd be back at the office." He gestured over his shoulder. "I can see if I can get you one."

"Would you?" Monica gave him her most persuasive smile.

They waited until Buddy and his ATV had receded into the distance before getting out of the car.

"Do we knock?" Greg kicked at a stone on the path. "What if Wilma doesn't answer? Assuming Wilma is the one using the cabin."

"Then we try the door and pray it's not locked."

Monica rapped sharply on the door and they waited. "She's not going to answer it," Monica said after several minutes. She reached for the door handle and turned it. "It's not locked."

"Do we just burst in?"

Monica was already easing the door open. She stuck her head through the opening. "Hello? Hello? Anybody here?"

There was a rustling sound near the open door to the small bathroom. Monica got a glimpse of the back of a gray sweater and a pair of black leggings.

"I didn't see her face, but I think it's Wilma."

"What if it isn't?" Greg whispered.

"We have to take that chance. You can give them your best smile and apologize."

Greg snorted.

Monica pushed the door open all the way and walked into the cabin. "You call her. Maybe she'll listen to you."

"Okay. Here goes nothing." Greg squared his shoulders. "Wilma? If that's you, please come out."

No response.

"Try again."

"Wilma. We're worried about you. Please. If you're in there, let us know you're okay."

The door opened a crack, then all the way and Wilma slowly walked out, a sheepish expression on her face. She stared at Monica and Greg for a moment and then began to cry.

Monica went to her, put her arms around her and patted her back.

"I was afraid you'd suspect me of Winslow's murder," Wilma said between sobs. "I didn't have anything to do with it. He was still alive when I left the fundraiser." She peered at Greg for a moment then put her head down again. "And I was embarrassed about . . . about what I did."

"So, you weren't kidnapped?" Monica said.

Wilma lifted her head and looked at Monica. "Kidnapped? What do you mean?"

"We received a ransom note asking for money for your release."

Wilma was already shaking her head. "No. How could that be? I came here on my own. Nobody forced me."

"Who else knew you were here?"

Wilma looked from Monica to Greg and then back again. "No one.

I mean, no one except Buddy. He let me use this cabin. He's the caretaker here."

"We've met Buddy." Greg loosened his scarf. "But no one else? You're sure? No one else knew you planned to disappear?"

Wilma shook her head. "You really were worried about me?"

"Yes. Both of us were."

"I don't imagine you want me to work for you anymore." She looked at Greg with sad eyes.

"Don't be silly." Greg patted her shoulder. "What would I do without you?"

"You mean it?" That resulted in a fresh torrent of tears, but eventually Wilma lifted her head and wiped a hand across her eyes. "I think I'd like to go home now."

• • •

Greg and Monica were pulling out of the campground with Wilma following behind when they spotted Buddy headed toward the cabin. He waved a brochure at them as they passed by and looked disappointed when they didn't stop.

"What are we going to do about him?" Greg put on his blinker and they left the campground and turned onto the main road. "It seems obvious he had to have been the one to send those ransom notes."

"I'll call Detective Stevens as soon as we get home. She can deal with him."

"It is a relief to know Wilma is okay. I have to admit, I've grown rather fond of her in a peculiar sort of way." Greg checked his sideview mirror and pulled out onto the highway. "You don't think Wilma will get in any trouble, do you?"

"I hope not." Monica pulled down the visor. "All she did was go away without telling anyone. I don't think that's a crime. A bit inconsiderate maybe but not illegal."

"I don't think she had anything to do with Winslow's murder." Greg passed a slow-moving car and then pulled back into the right lane. "Do you?"

"No." Monica sighed. "I never really did. I don't have any idea who the killer is. And it seems as if Stevens doesn't either. Unless she's not saying." Monica looked out the side window at the trees flashing by. "So many people had a grudge against the man. I can't imagine what it must have felt like to be so hated."

"Something tells me he didn't care. Those people weren't important to him. As a matter of fact, I think the only thing that mattered to him was money."

"And power. I got the impression he loved wielding his power over other people."

• • •

Mick, Janice and Nancy were clustered around Monica Monday morning. Mick was leaning against the counter, his legs crossed, and Janice was standing with her arms folded over her chest as if warding off an attack, and Nancy was calmly nursing a cup of coffee.

"We have a new order from the Cranberry Cove Inn," Monica announced.

Mick raised an eyebrow. "Salsa or compote."

"Neither."

Everyone looked confused. "What then?" Janice scowled.

"Don't keep us in suspense," Nancy said dryly in between sips of coffee.

"The Cranberry Cove Women's Club is having their annual Christmas luncheon at the Inn. The restaurant manager wants everything to be perfect or, to put it in his words, he wants to knock their socks off. We discussed ideas and I suggested using sugared cranberries to decorate the dessert. The chef is making a special cake for the event."

Nancy frowned. "When do they want these?"

"By this afternoon. The chef will be baking the cake first thing tomorrow morning."

"Excuse me." Mick looked puzzled. "What are sugared cranberries?"

"A simple syrup of sugar and water is brought to a boil and left to simmer for several minutes. The cranberries are then added to the syrup, and stirred until they are all well-coated." Monica paused. "Then they are removed with a slotted spoon and allowed to dry for an hour or so. Finally, the cranberries are rolled in granulated sugar to coat. When they're done, the cranberries look as if they are frosted with snow." Mick gave her a blank look. "It's very pretty," she added.

Janice looked disdainful. "That seems like an awful lot of work for a cake decoration."

"Nonetheless, that is what the chef plans to do. Our job is to make the sugared cranberries." Monica clapped her hands. "Mick, can you bring over a crate of berries."

"I'll get a bag of sugar." Janice scurried toward the stockroom.

Monica poured water into a pan and measured out the correct amount of sugar. She let it boil for several minutes before adding the cranberries. Nancy helped remove the cranberries from the syrup and arranged them on a baking sheet to dry. After an hour, Nancy rolled them in sugar and laid them out to dry again. Monica meanwhile got to work on the first batch of cranberry-walnut bread.

By the time Monica had eaten a sandwich for lunch, the cranberries were dry and ready to go. She carefully packed them in a box and carried them out to her car.

A light snow was falling when she reached downtown Cranberry Cove. A dusting covered the lights wound around the lampposts and had settled on the wreaths decorating the shop doors. The skies had darkened, and despite the hour, the streetlights were going on.

Not for the first time, Monica thought how magical Cranberry Cove was. Every season brought something new — flowers overflowing the hanging baskets in the spring, boats with colorful sails bobbing on the lake in summer, brilliant red and orange leaves on the trees in the autumn and twinkling Christmas lights and decorations in the winter.

Monica pulled into the driveway of the Inn and found a parking spot. She'd arranged to deliver the cranberries to the restaurant manager and not the kitchen for fear the box might be lost in the pandemonium that always preceded a special event.

The restaurant manager greeted Monica in the lobby. "We can't thank you enough for helping us out with this rush order." She shook her heard. "When the pastry chef gets an idea in his head, there's no changing his mind."

"I'm glad we could help."

"This luncheon is extra special since the Inn's owner's daughter is the chair this year." She shifted the clipboard tucked under her arm.

"I'll be sure to send you a picture of the finished cake for your social media."

"Thank you." Monica hadn't even thought about that but Lauren would be thrilled to have something for the farm's Instagram and Facebook accounts.

Monica handed over the box and said goodbye. She was crossing the lobby when she spotted Chelsea coming out of the restaurant.

"Monica, how are you?"

Chelsea's face was brighter than it had been the last time Monica saw her. The dark circles under her eyes had been erased and her forehead was no longer creased in worry.

"Are you leaving? I'll walk with you to your car," Monica offered.

"The money we raised at the fundraiser has really come in handy. I've been working with the architect on a scaled-down version of the addition I'd been hoping to build." She stopped next to a green Volkswagen Beetle. "Everything came together so well. The setting was wonderful and people enjoyed all the extras — the hot chocolate with all the trimmings, the live reindeer."

"The reindeer were a wonderful touch. How did you find Jason Vale?"

"I didn't. It wasn't me. I asked Sharon and some of our volunteers and no one had arranged for him to bring his reindeer. He just showed up."

That's peculiar, Monica thought as she said goodbye and headed to her own car. Why would Vale do that? Was it out of the goodness of his heart or did he have some other, more sinister reason for showing up and the fundraiser was just an excuse?

Chapter 21

Monica was about to get into her car when she decided to stop in and see Greg. She wondered if Wilma was back at work or if she was still recovering from her ordeal?

She left her car in the Inn's parking lot and began to walk down Beach Hollow Road to Book 'Em. As was so often the case in Michigan, the snow had stopped and the sun was trying to peek through a break in the clouds. The waves on Lake Michigan were momentarily stilled and frozen in place and a shelf of ice extended out into the water.

It was still well below freezing and Monica was glad when she walked into Book 'Em. She basked in the warmth for a moment, her numb fingers and toes slowly thawing out.

"This is a nice surprise." Greg took her hands in his. "You're freezing. Let me get you a cup of coffee."

He was heading toward the back room when Wilma appeared around the end of a row of shelves.

"It's good to see you back."

Wilma looked down. "It's good to be back." She bit her lower lip. "I talked to Detective Stevens. She was very understanding."

Monica put a hand on Wilma's arm. "That's good."

"I didn't mean any harm. My cell phone wasn't getting any service so I had no idea so many people were looking for me." She ducked her head again. "I didn't think I'd be missed."

"Of course you were missed. We were all worried about you."

"I didn't know Buddy was sending those ransom notes. Will he get in trouble? He was only helping me out."

"I don't know. I suppose we'll find out soon enough."

Greg returned with Monica's coffee and she cradled the cup in her hands gratefully. They still hadn't completely warmed up and the warmth felt heavenly. A customer approached Wilma with a question and the two of them drifted away toward the display table.

Monica sipped her coffee and was headed to the stockroom, when a woman came around the corner of the shelves and nearly collided with her. She put both hands around her mug to steady it. Monica frowned. "Angela Winslow, right? We met when I came to your house."

"I remember." She had two used paperbacks in her hands. "You were asking me about George. May he not rest in peace." She gave a laugh that sounded more like a cackle. "Good riddance to him. All he ever did was cause pain and misery to the people around him. He'd toy with them like a cat toys with a mouse. And then he'd discard them when they were no longer of use to him."

Monica didn't know what to say. Something had set Angela off, that was obvious.

"Like that one fellow who'd been at WinGeo for I don't know how long. He was the one who discovered Geosinex still contained codeine in its over-the-counter cough syrup even though it had been outlawed. He pointed it out to his boss and eventually it made its way up to George. George fired him. Called him a whistleblower."

"Do you know who that man was?"

Angela shook her head. "No. At least I don't remember now, assuming I ever did know his name." She glanced at Monica's empty coffee mug. "I should let you go. Nice seeing you." She made her way to the checkout counter.

Monica was left pondering. Angela obviously still harbored strong ill feelings toward Winslow. Strong enough to resort to murder? And does that whistleblower she mentioned have anything to do with his death? For every question answered, another one seemed to pop up.

• • •

All the way back to the farm kitchen and all through the afternoon, Monica thought about what Angela had told her about the WinGeo whistleblower. Who had it been? And were they still alive? The question teased her as she rolled out dough, filled muffin tins and took cookie sheets in and out of the oven. By the time she got home, she'd given herself a slight headache. Seeing Teddy and holding him again after the long day slowed her racing mind as she snuggled him and rubbed her cheek against his head.

Monica put Teddy in his carry cot and began making dinner, sautéing some diced carrots and onions for chicken soup, when Greg arrived home. He greeted Monica with a kiss on the cheek.

"How was the rest of your day?" Monica stirred the mixture in the pot.

"Very busy. People are beginning to realize Christmas is around the corner. The latest bestsellers—Lee Child, Harlan Coben, John Grisham—are flying off the shelves. Cozy mysteries are selling like crazy too. I'm going to have to reorder titles by a number of authors. Especially the ones with the holiday season as a theme."

"At this time of year, I think people enjoy something cozy." Monica added a carton of chicken broth to the pot and stirred it. "I ran into George Winslow's ex-wife today. She told me an interesting story about a whistleblower at WinGeo. It had to do with their cough syrup Geosinex. Remember, there was a medicine bottle lying near the body? What if the killer was trying to send some sort of message?"

Greg got a wineglass from the cupboard. "Want some?"

"Sure."

He grabbed another glass, filled them both and handed one to Monica. "But now that Wilma is back safe and sound and your friend Chelsea no longer seems to be a suspect—at least she hasn't been arrested yet—it's no longer your concern. You can leave it up to Stevens."

Monica made a face. Greg went over to her and put his arms around her. "Please? It could be dangerous. You might be walking into a spider's nest."

Monica took Greg's face in her hands. "I think you mean viper's nest."

"Either way, it might be dangerous. You've been lucky so far. What if your luck runs out this time?"

• • •

Monica couldn't let it go. She felt guilty, but certainly doing some online research couldn't be considered dangerous. She set her laptop up on the kitchen table and powered it on. She was scrolling through numerous articles on WinGeo, profits up, profits down, new vice president and so forth. She sighed. So far, she hadn't found anything relevant and she had to admit she was disappointed.

She laughed to herself about Greg using the expression "walking into a spider's nest." She pictured herself caught in a spider's web and shivered. She'd walked into spiderwebs before and she hated the sensation of the strands clinging to her hair and tickling her face.

There was something about spiders she should be remembering though. What was it? The thought kept eluding her no matter how hard she tried to grasp it. She was about to put her laptop away when it came to her. Jeff had been bitten by a spider when he was getting logs from the wood pile for the firepit at the fundraiser. She'd forgotten to ask him if it was healing okay.

There was something else, though, besides Jeff's spider bite. She turned her laptop on again and began searching. It didn't take her long to find numerous pictures of spider bites in various stages of healing. They looked just like the bite on Jeff's arm.

And they also looked like the red mark she'd recently seen on someone else's.

• • •

Monica had one thought on her mind when she woke up the next morning. Who did she know who used to work at WinGeo? Or, who knew someone who had been employed there and might know about the whistleblower? She knew her mother didn't. She hadn't been in Cranberry Cove long enough. She'd ask Janice when she got to the farm kitchen, but she doubted Mick would be of any help.

The contract with Cucina Italiana had arrived that morning in her email. She'd signed it and sent it back. They wanted the salsa as soon as possible, so they were going to have to get busy. She might even need to hire another part-time worker to help out.

"Good news," she announced when she got to work. Mick, Nancy and Janice all stopped what they were doing and stared at her. "I've signed the contract with Cucina Italiana, so it's official. We are going to be supplying them with our Sassamanash Farm salsa." She waited while everyone clapped. "And we're going to have to hustle."

"We hustle now as it is," Janice said under her breath.

Monica felt panic run through her. Was Janice so dissatisfied she might quit? That would be a disaster. She was an excellent baker and very reliable. First Mick and then Janice. She couldn't run the kitchen without them. The success of her little enterprise was due in great part to them. She'd have to think of a way to thank them and she'd look into the farm's budget to see if there was room for a small raise. And perhaps a Christmas bonus.

Monica looked at Janice. "You don't happen to know anyone who worked at WinGeo?"

Nancy frowned. "You're not investigating that murder, are you?" She sounded alarmed.

"Don't worry. I'm only doing some research. Nothing dangerous."

"You've said that before and you've nearly been killed how many times now?" She shook her head.

"You know what they say. A danger foreseen is a danger half avoided," Janice said with a smug expression.

Monica gave her mother's shoulder a squeeze. "Don't worry. I assure you this isn't dangerous." She could tell by the look on her mother's face that she didn't believe her but she had to see this through.

They worked diligently side by side and soon had enough product to take to the farm store. Monica loaded everything onto the cart. "I'll take this down to Nora." She slipped on her coat. It felt good to get out into the fresh air. The kitchen had quickly heated up with the oven going full blast.

Monica trundled the cart down the worn path to the farm store, which Jeff had given a fresh coat of paint over the summer. The bells on the wreath jingled as Monica opened the door. Nora helped her ease the cart through the doorway and they quickly began filling the case with cranberry bread, scones, muffins and more.

"I can't believe it's almost Christmas," Nora said as she arranged a dozen cookies on a paper doily atop an antique silver stand. "I have to get over to Bart's to reserve a standing rib roast for our dinner. My mother-in-law is spending the day with us and she loves a good roast, although I'm always so nervous hoping it comes out to her liking." She took a basket from the cart and began taking out the scones. "Of course, Bart's meat is always so good it's almost impossible to ruin it."

Monica couldn't help but smile. "And you know Bart will tell you exactly how to prepare it."

Nora chuckled "And he's always right."

"He'd agree with you."

Monica put the last of the loaves of cranberry bread in the case and stood back to admire the effect. She glanced at the cart. "Looks like that does it."

She was getting ready to wheel the cart to the door when she had a thought. It was a long shot, but what did she have to lose? "You don't happen to know anyone who worked at WinGeo, do you?"

Nora paused as she pulled off her gloves. "The pharmaceutical company? As a matter of fact, I do. My brother-in-law recently retired from there."

"Do you think he'd be willing to talk to me?"

"I don't see why not. But what's this about WinGeo? Didn't that company belong to the man who was killed here at the farm?" Nora paused. "You're not investigating, are you?"

"Just checking into a few things."

Nora raised an eyebrow. "Really?" she said dryly. She reached under the counter and pulled out a pad of paper and a pen. She scribbled on it. "Here's my brother-in-law's name and telephone number." She ripped off the sheet of paper and handed it to Monica. "Now that he's retired, he has a lot of time on his hands. Too much time according to my sister. I'm sure he'd welcome the distraction."

Monica looked at the paper, where Nora had written Henry Sanders and a telephone number.

She felt a stirring of excitement. She had the feeling that after going down numerous blind alleys, she was on to something at last.

• • •

Monica felt guilty leaving Mick to clean up the farm kitchen but he swore he didn't mind. She wanted to zoom into town to do some more Christmas shopping. She was almost finished and then she'd have to start wrapping the gifts. It wasn't her favorite occupation. It made her feel all thumbs. She always cut the paper the wrong size for the box and her folds weren't particularly neat. But it was the thought that counted, she reminded herself.

Cranberry Cove was buzzing with shoppers who obviously felt the fast approach of Christmas Day. She parked and locked her car and joined the parade of people going up and down the sidewalk, shopping bags swinging from their arms.

Lauren was next on her gift list and Tempest had said she was getting in some lovely crystal jewelry. Monica decided to take a look.

A gentleman in a dark gray overcoat was leaving Twilight when Monica got there. He held the door for her and wished her a merry

Christmas. The shop was warm and she loosened her scarf and unbuttoned her coat as she approached the counter. Tempest was busy rearranging a display of jade, topaz and rose quartz worry stones in the display case. She looked up and smiled when she saw Monica.

"You look very happy." Monica leaned against the case.

"I am. Do you remember what I told you about Emery? That I thought he'd never settle down? All he did was work, work, work. How was he going to find a girlfriend if his nose was always to the grindstone?"

"Something happened? Did he find someone?"

Tempest fiddled with the crystal on the silk cord around her neck. "It's early days yet so I shouldn't get my hopes up, but he's gone out several times with that woman who runs the animal shelter."

"Chelsea? That's great."

How wonderful if Emery and Chelsea connected, Monica thought. She knew Chelsea was lonely and suspected Emery must be too, even though he might not realize it since he worked so hard. Having met Greg had changed Monica's life for the better. Her life was now full and she wished everyone could be as lucky as she was.

Tempest sighed. "It may not last, but at least it's a start. He's coming out of his shell." She let the crystal drop back against her chest. "I'm sure you didn't come in here to talk about Emery. What can I do for you?"

"I'm looking for a present for Lauren. You said you were getting in some crystal jewelry."

"Yes." Tempest led her to the other end of the display case, where necklaces, earrings and rings were laid out on a black velvet background. "Something like this?" She pointed to a stone hanging from a delicate silver chain.

She removed it from the case and arranged it on a plush display pad. She pointed to the stone. "Topaz. It's meant to bring joy and abundance and promote creativity."

"That's perfect for Lauren." Monica ran her finger over the stone. She frowned. "How much is it?"

Tempest gave her the price and added, "I'll give you a discount of twenty percent. How is that?"

"That's too kind."

Tempest waved a hand. "My pleasure." She picked up the necklace. "I'll get this ready for you." She removed a small white box from a shelf, nestled the necklace on the square of cotton inside and added a sticker to the top of the box with her shop's half-moon logo.

Monica glanced at her watch. "You must be getting ready to close. Has it been busy?"

"So-so. I had two women in a while ago. The one almost couldn't stop complaining to her friend about her ex-husband, now late husband — the gentleman who was killed up at your farm — long enough to look at the merchandise." Tempest slipped the box into a bag. "She said she'd wanted to kill him and she wasn't sad he was dead."

As Monica left the shop she couldn't help wondering, had Angela merely fantasized about killing her husband or . . . had she actually done it?

Chapter 22

Monica was anxious to call Nora's brother-in-law, Henry. Teddy was napping when she got home. She went upstairs to the nursery and peeked into his crib. She felt a peculiar pain in her heart. She loved him so much it almost hurt. She tiptoed out of the room and tiptoed back downstairs.

She pulled her cell phone from her purse, set the baby monitor on the kitchen table and dialed the number Nora had given her for her brother-in-law.

A gruff voice answered the telephone. Monica introduced herself and asked if they could meet after dinner. He said yes without hesitation and they set a time. Greg would be home by then and could watch Teddy. She doubted she'd be gone long.

She took the container of pea soup out that she'd had in the freezer. Erwtensoep, as the Van Velsens called it. A Dutch favorite. She'd made the soup and frozen it knowing that she would be busier than usual as Christmas approached.

With dinner taken care of, she got the wrapping paper and ribbon she'd bought out of the closet and set them on the table. The trick now was to find the tape. Every year it seemed to wind up in a different place.

She opened the junk drawer in the kitchen and rummaged around. No tape. She blew out a breath in frustration and the curl that had fallen onto her forehead fluttered. They had a desk in the corner of the living room under one of the side windows. She looked through the drawers and finally found the tape dispenser.

She decided to start with Lauren's present, got it out of the Twilight bag and put it on the table. She had three rolls of paper and studied them carefully. She thought perhaps the one with the Christmas scene—pine trees covered in snow, an old-fashioned sleigh being pulled by a horse and a bright star in the sky—would suit Lauren.

She measured carefully and cut a piece of paper from the roll. She laid the box on it and breathed a sigh of relief when it turned out to be the right size. She was tying the ribbon into a bow when Greg arrived home. Waves of cold came off of him and his nose was red, as if it had been nipped by frost.

Teddy began to cry. "I'll get him." Greg went up to the nursery to get him while Monica microwaved the soup. She put out a bowl of croutons she'd made from some leftover bread on the table along with place mats and napkins.

Finally, Teddy was settled in his carry cot and she and Greg were able to sit down to dinner. She ladled the soup into thick pottery bowls and handed one to Greg.

"I see you've started wrapping. I saw there was a present under the tree."

"One lone present so far. It's for Lauren. I bought it at Twilight, a lovely topaz crystal on a silver chain." Monica stirred some croutons into her soup. "Tempest told me that George Winslow's ex-wife, Angela, had been to her shop. She was complaining about Winslow to the friend who was with her. She even said she'd wanted to kill him."

Greg's eyebrows shot up. "You're not taking that seriously, are you?"

"Why not?"

"People say things like that all the time without actually meaning them. Sort of a figure of speech."

Monica dropped her spoon into her bowl. "I don't know. When I talked to Angela, she was still full of anger, especially since he recently refused to up her alimony."

"I sure would have hated to be George Winslow." Greg wiped his lips with his napkin. "It sounds like he had more enemies than friends. If that's what having money does to you, I say no thanks."

Monica smiled at him. "We have everything we need."

Greg helped her clear the dishes and load the dishwasher.

"Do you mind watching Teddy while I go out?" Monica dried her hands on a towel.

"More Christmas shopping?"

"Not exactly. I'm meeting Nora's brother-in-law. He may have some of the information on WinGeo that I've been trying to track down."

"Be careful," Greg called after her as she went to get her coat.

• • •

The sky looked as if someone had stretched a piece of black velvet over its expanse and studded it with sparkling diamonds. Monica paused by her car for a moment to admire it. She took a deep breath of fresh air. She relished the pureness of it. There was no smell of the car exhaust that always hung in the air in Chicago.

Henry Sanders didn't live far and it wasn't long before Monica pulled into his driveway. The modest Cape Cod house was tucked into a cul-de-sac and was decorated for Christmas with colored lights strung on the bushes and a blow-up Santa in the front yard. Monica walked up the front path and rang the bell.

"You must be Monica," the woman who opened the door said. "I'm Maggie, Nora's sister." Maggie was an older version of Nora with short snowy white hair and the same vivid blue eyes as Nora, but Maggie was round where Nora was spare.

"I hope I'm not disturbing you." Monica stepped inside.

"Not at all. Henry has been looking forward to meeting you. Nora's told us all about the farm and those delicious goodies you make. She brings us some occasionally and I can't resist even though I know I should." She patted her stomach.

The foyer was as cozy as the outside of the house with a hooked rug on the wood floor and a colonial-style console table neatly stacked with mail.

Maggie led Monica into the living room, a comfortable space with two recliners facing a large-screen television and a camelback sofa piled with throw cushions and draped with a patchwork quilt. A chest of drawers had obviously been pushed to the side to make room for a Christmas tree that scraped the ceiling and was decked out with colored balls and dripping with silver tinsel.

Monica had always loved the long strands of tinsel but their tree had been an artificial one and her mother had said the tinsel was too tedious to remove when Christmas was over. She always insisted on the tree being taken down the day after Christmas and the living room furniture put back in its rightful place no matter how much Monica pleaded with her to leave it up a bit longer.

Henry got to his feet as they entered and extended his hand to Monica. His palm was rough but his grip was still strong. His eyes were as blue as his wife's and he was wearing loose-fitting jeans, suspenders and a plaid flannel shirt.

He motioned Monica to a seat on the sofa and collapsed back into his recliner.

"I'll make some tea, shall I?" Maggie didn't wait for an answer but bustled from the room.

Monica heard water running and dishes rattling in the kitchen.

Henry folded his hands across his stomach. "Now, what was it you were wanting to talk to me about? Nora told Maggie it was something about WinGeo." He moved and his chair creaked. "Sad about George Winslow."

Monica leaned forward with her hands clasped between her knees. "You liked him?"

"I don't know about liked. I had very little to do with him. There were a number of layers between me and the C-suite. Assistant managers, managers, directors and so on." He steepled his fingers. "He was ruthless. I do know that. I guess you have to be to succeed in business. I never did have it in me but Winslow was cutthroat in business and, I gather, in his personal life. He was on his second wife and the scuttlebutt was that he was eyeing a third."

"I heard something about a whistleblower . . ."

Henry lowered his bushy gray eyebrows. "So, you've heard about that. They tried to keep it quiet but we all knew about it. News travels fast on an assembly line. We took it as a warning to keep our mouths shut and our minds on our work."

"Do you know who this whistleblower was?"

"I didn't know him. He worked in quality control. That's how he found out what WinGeo was doing."

Please remember his name, Monica prayed to herself. "Do you know his name?"

Henry closed his eyes. "It was something-or-other Vale. Let me think." He suddenly sat forward with his elbows on his knees. "Walter, that was his name. Walter Vale."

Monica tried not to gasp. How common a name was Vale? Could Walter Vale possibly be related to Jason Vale?

"Do you know what happened to Walter Vale?"

Henry shrugged. "There were rumors that he took up drinking but I don't know much more than that, I'm afraid."

• • •

Monica woke up Wednesday thinking about Jason Vale. Was Walter Vale related to him? His father? Uncle? It wasn't a particularly common name. There had to be a connection between the two.

They had a busy morning ahead of them. Jason Vale's apothecary was having a grand opening late that afternoon and Sassamanash Farm was providing the food—cranberry-orange cookies, cranberry coffee cake and bite-sized cranberry scones. The Cranberry Cove Inn was catering the hot hors d'oeuvres and the drinks.

They were halfway through the morning and sweat was beading on Monica's forehead as she, Mick and Nancy pulled sheet after sheet of cookies from the oven. They sent the bare minimum of product down to Nora for the farm store. Monica told her to put out the *Closed* sign when things ran out. What Vale was paying them would more than make up for any lost customers.

By noon, Monica's car had been loaded with the delivery for Vale's apothecary. Monica briefly stepped into the restroom to splash water on her face and run a brush through her hair. She stared at her reflection in the mirror and wiped a blob of batter off her nose that she'd somehow missed.

Mick offered to go with her to help with the unloading but Monica felt confident she could handle it herself.

She double-parked in front of Vale's store and popped open the trunk. A banner with *Grand Opening* on it was strung across the shop window, fluttering in the breeze. Vale came out the door pushing a cart and he and Monica loaded everything on it and wheeled it into the store.

Shelves hanging from the wall behind the counter were lined with jars, the contents neatly labeled. A portable table had been set up in the middle of the space and was draped with a white tablecloth. Monica studied it for a moment and then began to arrange the cookies, slices of cake and scones on the disposable serving trays she'd bought for the occasion. The farm had done very little catering in the past and she wondered if they should look for more jobs like this.

"That's perfect," Vale said, eyeing the display. He was repeatedly rubbing his fingers over a fading red spot on his arm and Monica wondered if he was nervous.

"I understand your father used to work at WinGeo," Monica said, straightening one of the platters. "At least I'm assuming it's your father. Vale isn't all that common a name. I was told that Walter Vale was very brave and blew the whistle on some illegal practices."

Vale looked startled. It took him a couple of seconds to answer. "Yes, he did. I was very proud of him."

"I heard he was fired. I hope he landed on his feet."

"He's doing great. He got another job that paid better but he's retired now. He's in his eighties. Moved down to Florida. Said Michigan winters were becoming too much for him."

"I don't blame him."

"I hope you'll be coming back later," Vale said as they walked toward the door.

"Of course. I'd love to."

• • •

Monica thought she ought to change before heading to Vale's open house. She had flour on her sweater and had wiped her hands on her jeans more than once—a habit that infuriated her mother, who would always point out that that was what towels were for.

The open house started at three and went until five. Monica planned to arrive approximately midway through the event and Greg would join her if he could.

She'd left the farm kitchen early and she realized she had more time than she needed. It didn't take long to change into her good slacks and a nice blouse. Teddy was napping so she set up her laptop and went through her emails. It didn't take long. She drummed her fingers on the table. She'd done research on WinGeo but she hadn't found any articles about a whistleblower. Had she missed them or had WinGeo suppressed the information.

She started by typing Walter Vale's name into the search engine. That ought to narrow her search somewhat. A string of links came up almost immediately. She clicked on the first one and gasped. It was Walter Vale's obituary. What on earth . . . ?

Maybe it was a different Walter Vale, she reminded herself. The odds were that there was at least one other Walter Vale in the world. It didn't mean it was Jason Vale's father.

But it was. She began reading and soon discovered that they were one and the same. The obituary mentioned his employment at WinGeo and that Jason was his son.

Why on earth had Vale lied to her?

Chapter 23

All the lights were blazing when Monica arrived at Vale's apothecary. A balsam wreath on the front door and electric candles in the window added a welcoming touch. A dozen people were already there, some talking to Vale and others cradling cups of punch and picking at the goodies Monica had arranged earlier.

The shop was spic-and-span with light glancing off the sparkling plate glass window and the shelves behind the counter in perfect order.

Monica's lunch had been sketchy—some ham and cheese she'd scrounged up in the refrigerator—and she was starving. She was helping herself to a slice of cranberry cake and a glass of punch when she noticed the Van Velsens standing in the corner and went to join them.

"What do you think about this apothecary?" Gerda took a sip of her punch. She and Hennie were wearing matching lavender wool dresses with pleated skirts and round white collars.

"I remember how up in arms everyone was when Twilight opened," Hennie said. "They called it the woo-woo store. Although I like Tempest Storm very much, I still wonder who needs all that stuff she sells?"

"But this is different." Gerda crumpled her cocktail napkin between her fingers. "It's medicinal."

"Of a sort." Hennie sniffed. "I can't imagine what old Doc Zylstra would think of it. He's probably rolling over in his grave. If penicillin couldn't cure it, he didn't want to know about it."

"I think Mr. Vale is very nice," Gerda said timidly. "And quite handsome." A flush colored her cheeks.

Monica glanced at Vale. She supposed he was good-looking. Tonight, he was wearing a black shirt buttoned to the neck and black slacks instead of his usual jeans and sweatshirts.

"We'll see." Hennie's tone was ominous. "There's something about him I can't quite put my finger on."

Monica looked around and noticed that Vale had finished his conversation with the couple he'd been talking to and had gone behind the counter. She hesitated. Should she ask him why he lied about his father? Perhaps he had a good reason for it, although she couldn't begin to imagine what that might be.

Vale looked up, saw Monica and signaled to her. It looked as if the decision had been made for her.

"Everything's going well, don't you think?" He gestured toward the food. "Your cranberry goodies have been a big hit."

"I'm glad." Monica drew circles on the counter with her finger. Finally, she said, "You said your father was retired and living in Florida, didn't you?"

"Yup. He's living *la vida loca*." A wary expression came over Vale's face. "Why?"

Just say it, Monica told herself. *Rip the bandage off quickly.* "Because I found his obituary online. I thought perhaps I'd misunderstood."

Vale's posture became defensive. "You must have. My father is alive and well, and like I said, retired and living in Florida." He looked at the crowd. "And now, if you'll excuse me, there are some people I need to say hello to."

That was odd, Monica thought. Walter Vale's obituary had appeared in a reliable newspaper. Had someone posted it in jest? Don't newspapers check? She remembered that when her grandmother died, the funeral parlor sent the notice to the newspaper and they were hardly likely to make a mistake.

Vale had to be lying. But why?

• • •

By four thirty, people were beginning to trickle out of Vale's open house, some carrying bags with *Vale's Apothecary* written in bold block letters. Monica thought she'd stayed long enough to be polite and began to gather her things together. Greg had texted that he wasn't able to make it after all. There'd been a rush of Christmas shoppers and Wilma wouldn't have been able to cope on her own.

Monica was about to head home when she changed her mind. She couldn't stop thinking about Vale's lying about his father. What purpose did it serve? And when she'd asked him, he'd only dug his heels in and repeated the lie.

Monica sat in her parked car drumming her fingers on the steering wheel. Who might be able to shed some light on it? She thought of Debra Winslow. It's possible she might have known Vale's father, or perhaps had heard Winslow talking about him.

She glanced at her watch. It was still early enough to pay her a visit. She started the car and began the drive to Debra's.

Several lights were on on the ground floor. Monica took that as a sign that someone was likely to be home. She was glad she was dressed nicely and not wearing what she thought of as her work clothes.

She was especially glad when Debra responded to her knock on the door. She was looking flawless with perfectly done makeup and hair attractively styled, as if she'd just walked out of the beauty salon. She had on an at-home lounging outfit with matching top and bottom in a cream-colored knit. The jacket was unzipped just enough to show off a tank top in navy blue.

Was she expecting company? Monica wondered. Perhaps Owen Evans was stopping by for dinner?

"Oh. You're Monica, right?" She turned her wrist and looked at her watch. "Can I help you with something?"

"I have a few questions. I promise it won't take long."

"You'd better come in." Debra motioned Monica through the door then closed it behind her. "Although I can't imagine what it is I could possibly help you with."

They stood in the foyer facing each other. She didn't seem inclined to invite Monica to sit down.

Debra put her hands on her hips. "So, what is your question?"

Monica's feet were killing her and she glanced longingly at the cushy sofa visible in the living room.

Debra hesitated. "I guess we might as well sit down." Her tone was begrudging.

Monica followed her into the living room and had to stifle a groan of relief as she sank into the plush sofa cushions. It felt wonderful to get off her feet.

Debra balanced on the edge of a chair as if she was going to bolt at any minute. Her hands were tightly clasped in her lap and her shoulders were rigid. "What do you want to ask me?" She ostentatiously peered at her watch again. Monica didn't know if she was expecting someone or was merely telegraphing the fact that she didn't want this to take any longer than necessary.

Fine, Monica thought. She'd skip the pleasantries and get right to the point.

"Do you know anything about Walter Vale? He worked at WinGeo and blew the whistle on something they were doing that was illegal. Your husband fired him for it."

Debra seemed to relax. Her hands unclenched and her shoulders softened. Monica wondered what she'd been afraid she would ask her.

"I remember Walter Vale quite well. He was passed over for a job in management—a position he wasn't even remotely qualified for, by the way—and took it out on George. The whole thing was a nonissue really but you know how it is when lawyers get involved. George had no choice but to let him go."

"According to his son, he is now retired and living in Florida, and by his estimation is doing great."

Debra laughed. "That sure surprises me. He was a total mess after George fired him. That job was his life. He started to drink, lost his house and more than once was picked up for DUIs." She fiddled with the gold chain around her neck. "One day he even came here. It was horrible." She put her hands over her eyes. "I didn't want to open the door but he was like a crazy man. He kept pounding and pounding. I was terrified. No one was home. I was all alone."

She closed her eyes as if she was reliving the scene. "I finally had to let him in. He wouldn't stop beating on the door and I couldn't bear it any longer. He demanded to see George. He claimed George owed him money and insisted it be paid. I told him he'd have to talk to George. I didn't know anything about it. I thought he was going to refuse to leave and I told him I'd call the police if he didn't. In the end, he finally did. He threatened to come back later but he never did, thank goodness."

"That's definitely a different picture than the one his son painted." Monica leaned back against the cushions. "But here's the mysterious part. Vale is insisting his father is alive and living in Florida, and yet I found Walter Vale's obituary online. I didn't doubt that it was the same Walter Vale."

"That is peculiar." Debra frowned. "But I'm afraid I can't help you. I have no idea whether Walter Vale is dead or alive and frankly, I don't care."

Chapter 24

Teddy was fussy when he woke up on Thursday morning. Was he teething? Monica wondered. She ought to know when babies get their first teeth. Why didn't she? Alice insisted Teddy would eventually settle down but Monica couldn't leave while he was so unhappy.

She walked him up and down the family room until his eyelids drooped once, twice and finally closed and he was sleeping peacefully.

The farm kitchen was already humming when Monica burst through the door, as if rushing would make up for lost time. She tossed her jacket toward the hook on the wall and grabbed an apron.

"We were getting worried." Nancy slapped some dough down on the counter.

Good heavens, she was only twenty minutes late. "Teddy was being fussy." Monica tied her apron strings.

"You can never tell, what with all that investigating you insist on doing. You could be lying injured somewhere for all we know." Nancy's lips tightened.

Monica decided the best thing to do was to let the subject drop. "I heard on the radio that it's going down to below zero tonight." She grabbed the flour and began measuring some into a mixing bowl.

Mick shivered. "I don't know if I'll ever get used to this cold. In Greece, it rarely goes below seven degrees Celsius. That's about forty-five degrees in your language." Mick turned to the shelf behind the counter and picked up a white envelope. "This was under the door when I came in. I assume it's for you."

Monica took the envelope. It was an ordinary white business-sized envelope. The front was blank. What was this, Monica wondered. Who was leaving her a note. Maybe it was Jeff? That idea was comforting and she slid her finger under the flap and ripped it open. A folded piece of paper was inside.

She smoothed it out. The contents were brief. There was just the one word written in capital letters.

STOP.

"What's wrong? You've gone all white." Nancy rushed to Monica's side.

"You're not going to faint, are you?" Janice's tone made it obvious she didn't approve of giving in to fainting.

Monica's hand trembled as she handed the paper to Nancy. Nancy read it and gasped.

"I told you all this sleuthing could be dangerous. I should never have let you read those Nancy Drew books when you were younger. They put ideas into your head." She took Monica's hand in hers. "Now promise me you're going to stop this nonsense and be sensible. Leave the detective work to the police."

Monica agreed but she knew in her heart of hearts she wasn't going to let it drop. She'd come this far, she was going to see it through.

• • •

"Dinner's in the oven keeping warm," Monica said when Greg finally got home. She set up a place for him at the table and fetched a plate while he hung up his coat. "You look bushed."

Greg gave a tired smile. "Long day. I had to restock a lot of books and take inventory so I could order more."

He collapsed into a kitchen chair as Monica dished out the beef stew she'd made. She debated telling him about the anonymous note. He looked so tired. She decided to let him finish his dinner first.

"That was delicious." He handed Monica his plate after he'd devoured the meal. She rinsed it and put it in the dishwasher.

"Let's go relax." She linked her arm through Greg's and led him into the family room.

But she couldn't stop thinking about the note. Was it fair to keep that from Greg? On the one hand, it would keep him from worrying, but on the other hand, it was a betrayal of sorts. They'd promised not to keep secrets from each other. Finally, she blurted it out.

"I got an anonymous note I think came from Winslow's killer."

"What?" Greg sputtered before Monica even finished talking.

She pulled the note from her pocket and showed it to him.

His face blanched. "You don't know who sent this?" He waved the note in the air.

"No," Monica said, even though an idea of who sent it was forming in her mind. "But I think I can guess."

Greg plucked the note with his finger. "You have to show this to Detective Stevens. And you have to do what it says. Stop. Stop stirring things up. Leave it to the police. Please."

Monica was torn. She didn't want to lie to Greg but she was sure she was close to a solution to Winslow's murder. She compromised. "I won't do anything dangerous. And I'll show Detective Stevens the note first thing tomorrow."

Greg looked far from convinced.

"Honest."

She hoped he'd let the subject drop, and after several minutes he picked up the television remote and turned on the TV. Monica was relieved. She settled on the sofa while Greg took his favorite armchair. They were momentarily interrupted by a rustling sound on the baby monitor but Teddy settled back down again without so much as a whimper.

"Do you want to watch the news?" Greg's finger hovered over the button on the remote.

"Sure." Perhaps it would take her mind off of things, Monica thought. At least, she hoped so. Everything was going around and around in her head like a loop.

The WZZZ meteorologist was standing in front of a large map giving the weather report. The cold spell was going to continue for the rest of the week and snow was in the forecast, she said, using a pointer to delineate areas on the map that had lit up. The report ended and the familiar WZZZ anchor came into view.

Monica was having trouble concentrating and her eyes were beginning to close. Suddenly, she jerked to attention. Detective Stevens was on camera speaking with a reporter.

"There's been an arrest in the murder of George Winslow," she said, her expression serious. "The alleged killer, Sharon Dort, has been taken into custody."

"What led to solving the case?" The reporter shoved the microphone in Stevens's face.

"I'm afraid that's all I can say at the moment." She turned away.

A picture of Sharon Dort being led away by two policemen flashed on the screen. Monica gasped. Her face was chalk white and her eyes looked like those of a frightened animal. The sign for the Cranberry Cove Animal Shelter was visible in the background.

She had to do something. It was all she could do not to jump up from the sofa and race to the police station. The police had it all wrong. Sharon had tampered with Winslow's hot chocolate. Monica had no idea what sort of crime that would be considered. But she did know Sharon wasn't a murderer.

And she was quite sure she knew who was.

Chapter 25

Monica tossed and turned all night and when she got up in the morning, she felt as if she hadn't slept at all. The look on Sharon's face in that picture they'd shown on the news had haunted her all night long. The poor woman must be scared to death. She knew what she had to do. She had to go talk to Detective Stevens about her own theory.

She was in a daze as she changed Teddy, fed him and put him in a clean onesie. She rehearsed what she was going to say to Stevens in her mind so many times she was getting it all garbled up. Alice's arrival was a breath of fresh air, with her customary breezy chatter momentarily taking Monica's mind off her impending visit to the police.

"My, but it's cold out there. It must be close to zero degrees. I'm sure your pond out back has frozen over. Do you and Greg ice skate? Before you know it, you'll be teaching Teddy how."

Monica tried to hide a shiver at the mention of the pond in their backyard. The pond had a murky past where terrible things had happened.

"Greg played ice hockey in college and he's been dying to get out there but he's been so busy. I'm not much of a skater myself."

"I used to love it when I was younger." Alice whipped off her coat and hat. "I'd race my brothers and I'd beat 'em too." She looked at Monica under lowered brows. "Are you okay?"

"Just a bit tired. I didn't sleep well."

"I can make you a cup of coffee."

"No, thanks. I really should get going."

Monica kissed Teddy goodbye and got out her coat. She wasn't looking forward to this talk with Stevens. No one liked being told they were wrong about something. Certainly not the police. But for Sharon's sake, she had to do it. No doubt the dogs at the shelter were already missing her. She just hoped that Stevens would believe her.

It started to snow on her way to the police station, snowflakes that sounded like frozen pellets hitting her windshield. Monica turned on her wipers, and when the windows began to fog up, she turned on the defroster as well. She still didn't love driving in conditions like these.

In Chicago when it snowed, she had the option of public transportation. She hadn't even needed to own a car.

She was rounding a curve in the road when her tires slipped and she began to skid. Her heart was pounding by the time her tires gripped the road again and she was able to control the car. The only good thing about the drive, she thought, was that it had momentarily taken her mind off her impending meeting with Stevens.

She parked the car, locked it and dashed toward the door of the police station. Despite hurrying, she felt the snow on her hair melting and dripping down her neck. She wiped her boots on the mat and walked over to the sergeant behind the desk. He looked at her with one eyebrow raised in a question mark.

"I'd like to speak to Detective Stevens if she's free."

The sergeant put down his pencil. He had a crossword puzzle book open on his desk. He picked up the phone, spoke briefly then jerked his head toward the door. "Go on down. Detective Stevens is in her office and she said she'll see you." He'd barely finished speaking before he picked up his pencil again and went back to his puzzle.

Monica walked down the hall, where various noises came from behind the doors—a telephone ringing, someone shouting and a radio blaring.

Stevens was behind her desk, which had been swept clear of the tottering piles of paper and folders that were usually strewn across the top.

"You're not leaving, are you?" Monica gestured toward the desk.

"No. Just cleaning up a bit." Stevens's expression was tight. "Sit down."

Monica pulled the chair closer and sat down.

"What can I do for you?" Stevens's chair squeaked as she leaned back.

"I have some information about the Winslow case."

Stevens's eyes widened. "Really?" She leaned forward.

"I saw you've arrested Sharon Dort. It was on the news last night."

"Yeah."

"She didn't do it."

Stevens barked out a laugh. "What makes you think that? Sure, you've been lucky and pegged killers before, but this time your luck may have run out. So, tell me. Why do you think Dort is innocent?"

"Because Jason Vale did it."

"What makes you think that? What's his motive?"

"Revenge. Vale's father, Walter, blew the whistle on some illegal practices at WinGeo. Winslow fired him and he went downhill after that. He became an alcoholic and eventually died."

"Okay. What else?"

"Vale showed up at the animal shelter fundraiser with his reindeer. Everyone thought someone else had arranged it but no one had. Vale just turned up."

"Go on."

"Vale had a spider bite on his arm. My brother had one just like it. Jeff said there was a spider's nest in the woodpile by the barn. Winslow was hit with one of those logs. It seems reasonable that Vale got the bite when he grabbed one of those logs."

"Anything else?"

"Vale tried to throw suspicion on Emery, Tempest's son. He claimed he saw Emery at the fundraiser but Emery was at a conference hours away. What other reason would Vale have had for lying?"

Stevens leaned her elbows on her desk and steepled her fingers. "Interesting. I'll get Vale in here for questioning asap."

"And you'll let Sharon Dort go?"

Stevens held up a hand. "Whoa. Not so fast. First, let me talk to Vale."

Monica got up from her chair and began to button her coat. "Merry Christmas."

"Thanks. You, too." Stevens stretched her arms overhead. "My sister, brother-in-law and niece and nephew are coming to town. Should be a good time. How about you?"

"Everyone is gathering at our house for Christmas dinner. Christmas Eve, Greg and I will enjoy being alone. I like to light the tree and some candles and just take a moment to breathe."

Stevens's phone rang. "Sorry," she mouthed as Monica went out the door.

• • •

The snow had increased by the time Monica left the police station, lashing against her windshield and making it hard to see. She found herself clutching the wheel and leaning forward, straining her eyes to see more than a few feet in front of her.

She was rounding a curve when her ancient Ford Focus began to cough and sputter. *Please don't die on me now,* she prayed. She'd had a tune-up just a few weeks ago. She remembered the mechanic slapping the hood and telling her the old girl, as he called it, was in good shape and ought to last a few more years.

With the expense of the new house and a new baby, they could hardly afford a new car, even if it was pre-owned, as they called used cars nowadays.

The car had slowed to a crawl despite Monica's pressing the gas pedal nearly to the floor. She knew so little about cars that it was frustrating. Was it overheating? Was that even possible in conditions like this?

She scanned the dials on her dashboard. The speedometer said she was going ten miles an hour. She might as well be standing still. Something caught her eye and she looked again. It was the gas gauge and the needle was quite clearly pointing to the big red E.

How on earth had she run out of gas? She'd filled the tank three days ago and the trips between her house and the farm and downtown Cranberry Cove couldn't have possibly taken that much gas. Was there a leak in her gas tank?

She managed to pull off to the side of the road before the Focus came to a complete halt. What to do? She could call Greg and he could bring her some gas. The thought of admitting she ran out of fuel made her cringe. Or maybe Gina? She wasn't likely to judge. She didn't want to bother anyone at the farm store. They were busy enough as it was.

Headlights coming toward her glowed brightly through the swirling snow. The car slowed and then pulled off the road in front of her Focus. The door opened and someone began to step out.

Monica breathed a sigh of relief but her relief was temporary because the man getting out of the car was Jason Vale.

Chapter 26

Monica thought of that line from *Casablanca*, "Of all the gin joints in all the towns . . ." Of all the people to come along while she was stranded, it had to be Jason Vale. What was she going to do? Act naturally. Vale didn't know she suspected him of murdering Winslow. How could he? She'd act the way she normally did, although that was going to be difficult with her heart pounding so hard it was sending blood rushing to her face and making it hard to breathe.

Monica consoled herself with the thought that it was natural for anyone to be agitated in a situation like this as Vale approached her Focus. She rolled down her window and he leaned into the car.

"What happened?" He smiled encouragingly.

"I think I ran out of gas. I never run out of gas. As soon as the tank hits one-quarter full, I head to the gas station to fill it up." She realized she was babbling and clamped her lips shut.

"I can drive you to the gas station. I'm sure they'll have a can so you can get a bit of gas to get the car there." He stepped back and peered at her car. "You're out of the way so I don't think your car poses any danger, otherwise I'd say you'd better get a tow."

Monica hesitated. "I wouldn't want you to bother."

Vale grinned. "It's no bother."

"I can call my husband." She reached into her pocket for her cell phone.

"I don't think that's a good idea."

She raised her head and found herself looking down the barrel of a gun. She gasped.

Vale opened her door. "You'd better get out." He motioned with the gun. Monica reached for her purse but he stopped her. "You won't be needing that."

Monica managed to get to her feet but her knees immediately buckled. Vale grabbed her arm and pushed her forward, his other hand on the small of her back. They hit a patch of black ice and she fell, nearly pulling him down with her, but he yanked her to her feet again.

Her mind was racing. She'd gotten out of tough situations before and surely she could do it again. *Think!* But her mind had gone blank and all she could think about was keeping her footing on the slippery ground.

"Winslow deserved it, you know. He was a wretched man. He used people and then threw them away like trash. My father worked for him for years and years and instead of being grateful for his discovering the problem, Winslow fired him. And stiffed him out of his pension. My father went into a tailspin, began drinking and eventually committed suicide."

"I'm sorry. But what does this have to do with me?"

"I knew you'd figured it out and I know you went to the police. That's where I siphoned off all the gas in your car. You got further than I expected. That car gets good mileage." He laughed. "Not that that will do you much good now."

His words sent chills down Monica's spine and her teeth began to chatter. What was he planning to do? Shoot her?

"By the way, how did you figure out I was the one who killed Winslow?"

"Once I discovered your motive—to avenge your father—things began to fall into place." *Keep him talking,* Monica thought. Maybe a car would come along and she could flag it down. "You lied about your father being alive and well in Florida. Why would you do that unless you didn't want me to discover your motive for the murder." Monica started to slip but she regained her balance. "No one arranged for you to bring your reindeer to the fundraiser. You just showed up and everyone thought someone else had hired you."

"Go on." Vale prodded her forward.

"And you had that spider bite on your arm. Jeff got a similar bite when he was retrieving a log from the woodpile by the barn, where he said a spider was nesting. Winslow was killed with a log so it didn't seem too far-fetched to think you'd been bitten by a spider when you'd taken a log from that same pile to hit Winslow over the head with."

By now they'd reached Vale's car. "It was my good luck that that woman drugged Winslow's hot chocolate. It made things so much easier for me."

Vale opened the door to the backseat and pointed, saying, "Sit," as if Monica was a dog. She gave a momentary thought to running but where would she go? So far, no other cars had driven past them.

Everyone was hunkering down inside and keeping warm while the storm raged outside. What she wouldn't give to be at home now, safe and sound, with Teddy in her arms.

Teddy! She couldn't let anything happen to her for Teddy's sake. The thought gave her renewed resolve.

Vale pulled two lengths of rope off the passenger seat, where they had been coiled like a snake.

"Put your feet out," he ordered.

Monica tried to kick him but he managed to catch and hold both her legs. In no time, the rope was wound around her ankles and tied in a knot.

"Now put your hands out."

Fighting was useless and Monica did as she was told, holding them out side by side as Vale circled the rope around her wrists. He grunted, picked up her legs, swung them into the car and slammed the door.

Vale got into the driver's seat and started the car. The wheels spun for a couple of seconds then gripped and he pulled onto the road.

"Where are we going?" Monica struggled to keep her balance on the backseat as the car went around a curve.

Vale glanced over his shoulder. "The lake."

"Why are you taking me there?" Monica tried to keep the wobble out of her voice.

"You'll see."

The snow had begun to let up and visibility was getting better. Vale stepped on the gas and they picked up speed.

A million thoughts whirled through Monica's head all at once. What was Vale planning to do? Would she find a way to escape? What would happen to Greg and Teddy if something happened to her?

She tried to distract herself by looking out the window. The road had narrowed and so far no cars had passed them. The landscape was desolate with the grasses alongside the road weighed down by ice and snow and the partially frozen lake a strip of silver in the distance.

Suddenly, Vale turned off the road into a lay-by, the car wheels churning up chunks of snow. He jerked to a stop and Monica fell forward, hitting her head against the back of the seat in front of her. She barely registered the pain in her panic over what Vale was planning.

Vale opened his door, got out and then yanked Monica's open. An icy blast of air rushed in and chilled the sweat forming on her forehead.

"Get out." Vale's mask of cordiality was gone now, replaced by the face of a ruthless killer. He held the gun loosely in his right hand.

Monica struggled to swing her legs out of the car but the rope around her ankles was making it difficult. Vale grabbed her arm and pulled her out. She hit her head again, this time on the roof of the car, but she barely noticed it. Her teeth were chattering and she was shivering uncontrollably.

"Let's go."

They made their way across the flattened grass and onto the stretch of sand leading to the lake. Progress was slow with Monica only being able to take mincing steps because of her bound ankles. The sand was a further challenge. It was hard to keep her balance and more than once Vale had to pick her up after she'd fallen.

Her fear mounted as they got closer and closer to the lake. What was he planning? How was she going to get out of this? She wished she had nine lives like cats supposedly do.

As they got closer to the water, she began to pull back. She pretended to fall more than once and each time Vale wrenched her to her feet more and more viciously, but despite her delay tactics they eventually arrived at the edge of the lake.

The water near the shore was frozen solid, with the ice forming a solid shelf reaching further out.

"The lake has only ever completely frozen over five times," Vale said, as if they were chatting at a cocktail party or were two friends having lunch. The ordinariness of the comment scared Monica even more. The man was heartless and possibly insane.

They took their first tentative step out onto the ice. Monica gritted her teeth, expecting to hear the ice cracking under them at any moment.

They inched their way along until Vale said, "This is good."

"Good for what? What are you doing?" Monica's teeth were chattering so badly her words were barely understandable.

"Get down." Vale pointed to the ice.

How? Monica thought. She needed her hands to brace herself. Vale began to grow impatient. Monica could tell he was as cold as she was. He wasn't wearing a hat and the tips of his ears were bright red and so was his nose.

"Come on." He gave her a shove. Her feet flew out from under her and she landed on her back on the ice. For a moment she was dazed and stared up at the sky, then she began to struggle trying to get back on her feet.

Vale crouched down and gave her another shove. It sent her sliding across the ice even closer to where it dropped off and the water began. She tried inching her way back to where Vale was standing but it was difficult and she made little progress.

"See you." Vale saluted, turned around and began walking back to the shore.

"Wait!" Monica shouted. "You can't leave me here." But Vale didn't even bother to turn around. He kept walking, leaving Monica trussed up and laying on the ice. She felt like Pauline, tied to the railroad tracks in *The Perils of Pauline.* She almost gave in to hysterical laughter but then the gravity of her situation hit her anew. How was she ever going to get free?

It was useless to hope that someone would come along and rescue her. So far, there'd been virtually no traffic and any driver would be focused on the road, not looking out over the lake. She rolled onto her stomach and managed to get into a kneeling position. She tried repeatedly to push herself to her feet, but each time she slid and ended up facedown again.

Then she heard a sound that chilled her even more than she already was. The sound of ice cracking.

Chapter 27

Monica felt a sense of overwhelming despair wash over her. She should have listened to her mother and to Greg and to everyone else who had told her to leave the investigating to the police. Then she wouldn't be in this pickle.

Ice cracked again and a piece broke off the very end of the frozen shelf. She had to do something. Fast. She remembered that news report about what to do if you were ever standing on a frozen lake when the ice began to crack. You needed to distribute your weight over the largest area possible by lying down. Which was fortunate since she was already prone on the ice.

Then you were supposed to roll toward the shore as quickly as possible. Monica remembered rolling down hills as a child and her mother getting all annoyed because she'd gotten grass stains on her clothes. It ought to be child's play. Or so she thought.

She tried to flip from her stomach to her back and it took more effort than she'd expected. It had been so easy when she was a kid. She glanced toward the shore. She had a long way to go.

She flipped again and again. When she felt she was safely on thicker ice, she took a moment to rest. She was actually getting heated up despite the frigid temperatures.

A few more flips and she was off the ice and on the sand. She lay there for a few moments gasping like a fish out of water. Unfortunately, she realized her ordeal wasn't over. Black clouds were massing on the horizon and soon it would be snowing again. She didn't know how much longer she'd be able to survive the cold.

She realized the rope around her wrists had some play in it. They chafed her skin but she bit her lip and managed to turn her hands so that her palms were facing each other, giving her enough wiggle room to begin easing her hands out of their bindings.

She managed to push herself to a sitting position and gratefully circled her wrists around and around to ease their stiffness. She looked back toward the road. No one had appeared to save her, unlike Pauline, who had had her share of rescuers. She was going to have to figure this out herself.

With her hands free, she ought to be able to undo the rope around her ankles. She began working on the knot but her frozen fingers were clumsy and she was making little progress. But she wasn't giving up. She clawed at the knotted rope until her fingers were raw.

For a moment, she was tempted to put her head down and cry, but then she thought of Teddy and running her hand over the sweet softness of his hair, his little hand curling around her finger, and she got a burst of energy.

Her hopes rose as the knot began to loosen and the rope started to fray. After working on it for several more minutes, the knot came undone and the rope unfurled from around her ankles. She circled her feet and wiggled her toes, trying to get some sensation back.

She had to get up off the frozen ground. She got to her knees and waited a moment to catch her breath before finally standing up. She made her way to the road, keeping an eye out for any cars, but there were none. She wasn't going to last much longer in these temperatures. She stomped her feet in an attempt to regain circulation and stuck her hands in her pockets for extra warmth.

Her fingers touched something and she realized it was her cell phone. She'd forgotten all about it. She prayed she would get service. She pulled it out and woke it up. One bar. Hopefully, that would be enough.

Her fingers were so stiff she could barely punch the button for her contacts. She scrolled until she found Greg's number and held her breath as she pressed the telephone icon. The call went through and it began to ring. One ring, two rings, three rings. Greg finally answered on the fifth ring.

He gasped when Monica told him what had happened. "Have you called 911?"

"I don't know where I am." A sob caught in Monica's throat. "It was snowing and I could barely see where we were going. How will they find me?"

"Did he drive north or south?"

"I was headed to the farm when he came along but he was going in the opposite direction."

"He didn't turn around?"

"No. We headed north. We drove for maybe twenty minutes before he pulled over by the lake. It's deserted here."

"Check that the location tracker on your phone is on then call 911.

They should be able to get your approximate position from the data. The police will get there faster than I could but I'll be on my way." He paused. "I love you, Monica. Everything is going to be okay."

Monica didn't want to hang up. Hearing Greg's voice was calming and reassuring and so ordinary she momentarily forgot where she was. But she knew what she had to do. She ended the call and dialed 911.

After talking to the dispatcher, Monica stood clutching her phone, straining to hear sirens in the distance. She began to feel very sleepy and it was tempting to lie back down and take a nap. She shook herself. She wasn't making any sense. What was happening to her? Her eyelids dropped and her chin fell to her chest. She was nearly asleep when there was a faint sound in the distance. She snapped awake and listened. Were those sirens? *Please, let those be sirens.*

The sound grew louder as it got closer. They were sirens. Monica prayed they were coming for her. She stared hopefully at the road until a police car skidded to a stop and two officers got out and ran toward her. Moments later, an ambulance appeared and parked behind the patrol car. Monica watched as two EMTs got out, opened the hatch at the back and pulled out a gurney.

The two policemen reached her and each took an arm. They supported her as they made their way toward the ambulance. She was barely conscious as the EMTs helped her onto the gurney, strapped her in and covered her with a mylar emergency blanket.

"Let's go," one shouted to the other. They slid the gurney into the back of the ambulance and secured it. The door slammed shut and Monica heard the siren sound as they pulled onto the road and began speeding toward the hospital.

After all that, was Vale going to get away? The thought tormented her all the way to the emergency room.

• • •

Monica dozed off and on during the ride to the hospital, jerking fully awake when the ambulance came to a stop in front of double glass doors with the word *Emergency* above them in large red letters. Greg was waiting for her and accompanied her as they wheeled her inside. She was taken into a cubicle and transferred from the gurney to a bed. Nurses came in and out, checking her blood pressure, taking her blood, hooking up an IV and bringing her warm drinks and something to eat. She hadn't even realized how hungry she was until she started to warm up.

She was finishing her turkey sandwich when Stevens popped her head around the edge of the curtain. "May I come in?"

"Yes. Of course. Is there any news?" Monica tried to sit up.

Greg jumped up and offered Stevens the only chair in the room but she shook her head. "I won't be long. I'm sure you need to rest." She was quiet for a moment. "I can't tell you how glad I am that you're safe." She shook her finger at Monica. "One of these days, you're going to stick your nose into police business and you're not going to be so lucky."

Monica nodded and looked down at her hands.

"We put out a BOLO for Vale and a couple of officers have already picked him up. He's not going to bother you again. Or anyone else, for that matter." Her phone rang. "Excuse me." She stepped out of the room. Several minutes later she stuck her head in again. "I've got to go." She waved. "Good job," she added before leaving.

The curtain was pushed aside again and a doctor walked in. She smiled at Monica and Greg. "Your vital signs are all good and there don't seem to be any lasting concerns, so you're free to go. The nurse will be in shortly with the discharge papers." She smiled again and left the room.

"It will be good to get home. For a while I was afraid I'd never get to be there again." Monica slipped out of her hospital gown and pulled on her jeans. They were still slightly damp and clung to her legs. She would change as soon as she got home. The vision of her warm robe and slippers and a seat in front of the fireplace spurred her on. "Everyone at the farm kitchen must be wondering where I've gotten to."

Greg held out her jacket. "No need to worry. I called them on the way here. They all send their love."

That thought warmed Monica more than anything and she allowed Greg to lead her out to the car.

• • •

"Here we are." Greg pulled into their driveway. He ran around the car and opened Monica's door. He put a hand out to help her, for which she was grateful. She was still a bit stiff from being trussed up like the Thanksgiving turkey.

Alice was waiting, her face creased with concern. "Thank heavens," she said when Monica walked in the door. "We were so worried."

As soon as Monica got upstairs to their bedroom, she removed her wet clothing and wrapped her robe around her and belted it tightly. She slipped her feet into her fuzzy slippers and went downstairs to sit on the couch. Greg had lit the logs in the fireplace and the flames leaped and spit, sending out welcome warmth.

She picked Teddy up from his carry cot and snuggled him against her shoulder, breathing in his soft scent.

"Do you want the television on?" Greg pressed the button on the remote. "Is the news okay?"

"Sure. Maybe there's something about Vale's capture."

Greg gave her a teasing smile. "I imagine that would give you great pleasure."

The television flickered on. The first story was about a recall of canned baked beans that had caused half a dozen cases of botulism across the country. The reporter's voice droned on and Monica felt her eyes closing. She was vaguely aware of Greg gently taking Teddy from her and putting him in his carry cot. He, too, was asleep.

A new story came on that jerked Monica awake. She rubbed her eyes and shook herself. Stevens was on the screen and a reporter in a black overcoat and paisley scarf was standing next to her. A chyron ran across the bottom of the screen that read *Suspect in Winslow Murder Apprehended.*

"This is Detective Stevens of the Cranberry Cove police." He gestured toward Stevens.

"Detective Stevens, can you fill us in on the murder of George Winslow, CEO of WinGeo Pharmaceuticals? I understand you just made an arrest. But hadn't someone already been arrested?" He thrust the microphone in her face.

Stevens scowled. "We had but it became clear upon examination of the evidence that person wasn't the perpetrator."

"You made a mistake?"

"Yes, but we identified who we believe to be the correct suspect in the murder of Winslow, and after a brief chase he was apprehended and taken into custody. Motive for the murder is not known at this time. We hope to have more details shortly."

She stepped away from the microphone, turned around and walked away.

The whole ordeal flashed through Monica's mind again and she began to shake.

"Are you cold?" Greg reached for the afghan. She shook her head. He crouched down in front of her and took her hands in his. "Do you want to tell me about it?"

Monica thought for a moment. "Not yet. I'm still processing everything. But soon."

• • •

Monica stood back and looked around the family room. The tree was lit, a fire was burning in the fireplace and the smell of puff pastry baking in the oven drifted in from the kitchen. She was ready.

She'd invited Jeff and Lauren, her mother, Gina, Estelle, Alice, Chelsea and everyone from the farm kitchen to a Christmas party to thank them for all their love and support.

She was pulling the sheet of appetizers from the oven when the doorbell rang. She whipped off her apron as she ran to open it.

"Merry Christmas," Gina and Estelle shouted. Gina handed Monica a bottle of champagne.

The two women had gone all out with sequined tops and wide-legged palazzo pants. They'd just walked through the door when Nancy and Janice arrived. Nancy was wearing a long red plaid skirt and white silk blouse and Monica was shocked to see Janice in a jaunty red Santa hat. When everyone had arrived, Monica handed out glasses while Greg popped open the bottle of champagne and filled them. Monica clapped her hands for attention. "Here's to Nancy, Mick, Janice, Nora and Alice, who have helped make Sassamanash Farm's cranberry goods such a success. From Nancy, who coined our new slogan Oven-Fresh Every Day, to Mick and Janice for being so reliable, to Nora for being so gracious to our customers and to Alice for taking such good care of Teddy when I'm working. I can't thank you enough. Cheers." She picked up her glass and raised it.

Janice insisted on helping pass around the hors d'oeuvres, although Monica told her it wasn't necessary and to relax. "The devil finds work for idle hands," she said as she took the tray of cranberry and brie puffs from Monica and began to circulate with them.

Chelsea followed Monica out to the kitchen when she went to fetch more cream cheese and cranberry compote dip.

"Need any help?"

Monica nodded her head toward the table. If you don't mind, that would be great. Can you arrange those crackers on the empty plate."

"Sure thing." Chelsea pulled a sleeve of crackers out of the box and tore it open.

Monica noticed Chelsea's face was much brighter than it had been. "You seem to be in the holiday spirit."

"I am." Chelsea's eyes twinkled. "I've been seeing Emery, Tempest's son." Her face colored bright pink.

Monica put down the spoon she was holding and gave Chelsea a quick hug. "I'm so happy for you."

Chelsea's smile broadened. "He loves dogs as much as I do. I'm going to visit him in Grand Rapids and I'll get to meet his dachshund, Max." A cloud passed over her face. "What's going to happen to Sharon Dort? Do you know?"

"I heard last night on the news that the judge sentenced her to three months of probation in light of her clean record."

"That's a relief. We've all really missed her. We depended on her more than we realized."

Monica finished replenishing the dip in the bowl and Chelsea took it from her. "I'll put this on the table."

"I'm glad they caught that awful man," Gina said when Monica walked back into the family room. She had finished her champagne and was drinking a glass of eggnog. She peered into it and sniffed. "Did you put anything in this?" she asked Monica.

Monica was puzzled. "What do you mean? It came in a carton already prepared."

Gina tapped her long red nails against her glass. "I mean brandy, rum, bourbon. Something to goose it up a little."

"No, I didn't."

"I'm going to get some of that whiskey you keep in the kitchen cupboard." She started to get up but Greg waved her back to her seat.

"I'll get it for you."

"I wonder what's going to become of Vale's apothecary?" Gina shook her head. "What a shame. He seemed like such a nice man."

Monica shivered. "Well, he wasn't," she said, a little more harshly than she'd intended. "He tried to kill me."

"It gives me chills every time I think about it." Nancy crossed her arms over her chest.

"Then don't think about it." Gina hid her smirk by taking a sip of her eggnog. Nancy shot her a look.

They weren't going to start fighting, Monica hoped. They'd been getting along so well. Things had been tense when Nancy had first arrived in town but eventually they'd reached a certain equilibrium.

"We have an announcement to make." Jeff put his arm around Lauren. Monica smiled at him, grateful for the distraction.

"Don't keep us in suspense." Gina tipped back the rest of her eggnog.

Jeff and Lauren looked at each other. "You tell them." Jeff prompted her.

Lauren's face turned rosy and took on a glow. "Jeff and I are going to have a baby." She looked at Jeff and he bent and gave her a peck on the lips.

"I'm going to be a grandmother," Gina shouted. She jumped up from her seat and went to hug Lauren and Jeff. She turned to the rest of the group. "I'm going to be a grandmother."

Everyone gathered around and took turns hugging the happy couple.

Monica turned to Greg. "Teddy is going to have a cousin."

As if on cue, a wail came from the baby monitor. "I'll get him." Greg headed toward the stairs.

"How about you and Greg?" Nancy said. "You don't want Teddy to be an only child, do you?"

Monica hesitated. She'd always wished she'd had a sibling and had been so thrilled when Jeff came along. Even though they were half siblings, it had felt as if she was no longer an only child.

Nancy was looking at her with a raised eyebrow.

"We'll see," Monica said. They'd have to be content with that for now.

About the Author

Peg grew up in a New Jersey suburb about twenty-five miles outside of New York City. After college, she moved to the City, where she managed an art gallery owned by the son of the artist Henri Matisse.

After her husband died, Peg remarried and her new husband took a job in Grand Rapids, Michigan, where they now live (on exile from New Jersey, as she likes to joke). Somehow Peg managed to segue from the art world to marketing and is now the manager of marketing communications for a company that provides services to seniors.

She is the author of the Cranberry Cove Mysteries, the Lucille Mysteries, the Farmer's Daughter Mysteries, the Gourmet De-Lite Mysteries, and also, writing as Meg London, the Sweet Nothings Vintage Lingerie series, and as Margaret Loudon, the Open Book series.

Peg has two daughters, a stepdaughter and stepson, and two beautiful granddaughters. You can read more at pegcochran.com and meglondon.com.

Printed in Dunstable, United Kingdom

72413504R00111